Laura Martin writes histo
an adventurous undercurre
she spends her time working as a doctor in
Cambridgeshire, where she lives with her husband.
In her spare moments Laura loves to lose herself in
a book, and has been known to read from cover to
cover in a single day when the story is particularly
gripping. She also loves to travel—especially to
visit historical sites and far-flung shores.

Also by Laura Martin

The Captain's Impossible Match
The Housekeeper's Forbidden Earl
Her Secret Past with the Viscount
A Housemaid to Redeem Him
The Kiss That Made Her Countess

The Ashburton Reunion miniseries

Flirting with His Forbidden Lady
Falling for His Practical Wife

Matchmade Marriages miniseries

The Marquess Meets His Match
A Pretend Match for the Viscount
A Match to Fool Society

The Cinderella Shepherd Sisters miniseries

One Waltz with the Viscount

Discover more at millsandboon.co.uk.

ONE FORBIDDEN KISS WITH THE LAIRD

Laura Martin

MILLS & BOON

All rights reserved including the right of reproduction in whole or in part in any form. This edition is published by arrangement with Harlequin Enterprises ULC.

This is a work of fiction. Names, characters, places, locations and incidents are purely fictional and bear no relationship to any real life individuals, living or dead, or to any actual places, business establishments, locations, events or incidents. Any resemblance is entirely coincidental.

Without limiting the author's and publisher's exclusive rights, any unauthorised use of this publication to train generative artificial intelligence (AI) technologies is expressly prohibited. HarperCollins also exercise their rights under Article 4(3) of the Digital Single Market Directive 2019/790 and expressly reserve this publication from the text and data mining exception.

® and TM are trademarks owned and used by the trademark owner and/or its licensee. Trademarks marked with ® are registered with the United Kingdom Patent Office and/or the Office for Harmonisation in the Internal Market and in other countries.

First published in Great Britain 2025
by Mills & Boon, an imprint of HarperCollins*Publishers* Ltd,
1 London Bridge Street, London, SE1 9GF

www.harpercollins.co.uk

HarperCollins*Publishers*, Macken House, 39/40 Mayor Street Upper, Dublin 1, D01 C9W8, Ireland

One Forbidden Kiss with the Laird © 2025 Laura Martin

ISBN: 978-0-263-34530-8

08/25

This book contains FSC™ certified paper
and other controlled sources to ensure responsible forest management.

For more information visit www.harpercollins.co.uk/green.

Printed and Bound in the UK using 100% Renewable Electricity
at CPI Group (UK) Ltd, Croydon, CR0 4YY

For my boys.
I can't wait for our next Scottish adventure.

Chapter One

Loch Leven—1817

Selina stood looking out over the murky water, mesmerised by the movement as the wind disturbed the surface and sent ripples in first one direction and then another. It was a cloudy night so there was no reflection of the moon or stars, just a deep, inky blackness that seemed to suck in all light.

The rain had started in earnest a few minutes earlier and now was stinging her face as if a thousand tiny needles were assaulting her. Never had she known cold like this. It wasn't even winter, yet the chill of the air penetrated through her many layers and made her shiver and shake. Normally she would run back to the house and warm herself by one of the roaring fires, but tonight Selina relished the cold as it seeped through her clothes. It reminded her she was alive. Besides, there was nothing to rush back for—

no one would miss her, or, if they did, they would be quietly thankful she was not there, an unwelcome outsider on this trip.

She sighed, wondering how she had been so stupid for so long. All she had wanted was a little bit of affection, a private acknowledgement that she *did* matter. She was the illegitimate child of Sir William Kingsley, abandoned along with her twin sister and her mother twenty-two years earlier. She hadn't ever asked for her father to publicly declare his relationship to her, but she had hoped… Her thought trailed off. She wasn't sure what she had been hoping for. She'd dreamed of tearful reunions and being swept into the heart of a loving family. She had fantasised about her father insisting she be recognised as his daughter and arranging a parade of desirable young men as her suitors.

Selina let out a half-sob, half-scoff. The reality had been very different. Hidden away, her existence barely acknowledged, treated like a disease-ridden beggar girl by her father's wife and legitimate daughter.

For some reason she had thought this trip to Scotland would be different. It had been a surprise when she had been invited and the naive part of her had hoped it might signal a softening towards her. Officially she had been introduced as a pauper distant relative, taken in to fulfil some light secretarial duties and also provide companionship to Catherine Kingsley, without ever letting on that Catherine was in fact her half-sister. Now she could see her father was just desperate to keep her quiet and the only way he could ensure she was not going around telling everyone the truth of her origins was if he kept her close.

Selina crouched down, letting her fingers trail over the surface of the loch. The water lapped against the bank here, dark and deep. She got the sense that if she fell in it would swallow her up, dragging her down into the abyss. That wasn't what she wanted. She wanted to be in the light, to twirl through the ballrooms of London, to parade with her head held high in Hyde Park.

Slowly she stood, wondering if she could find a new dream. Ever since she had discovered her father wasn't some obscure soldier, dead before she was born, her dreams had been centred around being accepted into high Society, a place she would never normally have been able to penetrate. Now she could see it was never going to happen. She needed a new dream, something different to strive for, but she did not know what that could be.

With a sigh she took one last look down into the darkness of the water, teetering on the edge of the loch. She spread her arms wide, allowing the wind to whip at her cloak, reminding herself that it was good to be alive, even if she was stuck in Scotland with people who despised her.

Callum Thomson paused, ignoring the wind and rain that whipped at his body. Extremes of weather were to be expected here and ever since he had returned to Scotland he had learned to appreciate the storms that battered his homeland. By his side Hamish waited patiently, alert for any possible danger, one ear cocked and one front paw raised, as if ready to dash after an invisible prey at any moment.

Visibility was poor in these conditions, but Callum's eyes were sharp and he knew these hills better than any other place on earth. Down by the edge of Loch Leven there was something out of place.

'Let's have a look, boy,' he said quietly to Hamish and together man and dog made their way towards the loch.

They covered the ground quickly, Callum's feet seeming to float over the uneven ground. When they were still about fifty feet away he saw the young woman standing, teetering on the edge of the loch and then spreading her arms wide.

His heart sank and he felt a rush of panic. In his opinion Loch Leven was one of the most beautiful places in the world, but in this weather there was a danger to it, a savagery that people could underestimate. It had claimed the lives of many over the centuries and most recently his father just ten years earlier. On a night not unlike tonight his father had thrown himself into the loch, giving in to the demons that chased him. Callum had been unable to do anything to save his father, but he would not let some other poor soul go the same way.

With a roar he ran as fast as he could towards the figure on the edge of the loch, deviating from the straight path between them and him only at the last minute so he could dive at them from the side without risking knocking them both into the cold water. He launched his body through the air and tackled the person to the ground, surprised when they toppled so easily, letting out a high-pitched shriek.

Callum landed on top of the woman, her elbow finding its way into his upper abdomen, knocking the air from his lungs. She lay motionless underneath him, her eyes wide and alert, but her body stunned.

For thirty seconds neither of them could move and then the woman began to wriggle, panic filling her eyes. Callum scrambled back, pushing himself to his feet and moving a little distance away. He wanted to reassure her that he was not there to hurt her, but he also did not want to move so far away that she could go ahead and launch herself into the cold water as she had seemed so intent on doing only a minute earlier.

'Don't do it,' he rasped.

She looked at him, her face a picture of incredulity.

'Don't do what?'

'Jump.'

For a moment it was as if his words did not register and he wondered if her mind was affected by the harsh conditions. He had seen many a hardy man lose his sense of reason if out in the cold and the wind for too long.

'Jump? I wasn't going to jump.'

He raised an eyebrow. 'Only a fool would stand so close to the edge of the loch if they weren't contemplating jumping in.'

'It is hardly the night for a swim.' She was regaining her colour now and some of her spirit, straightening her back and lowering her shoulders as she looked at him.

'Why did you attack me?'

He snorted. 'I didnae attack you. I saved your life.'

'My life was never in peril,' she said, jutting out her chin. She was petite with long brown hair that hung loose underneath the hood of her cloak. Her eyes were dark, perhaps brown or green, it was impossible to tell in this light, but Callum saw a spark of temper flare in them. He wasn't overly surprised—if someone had tackled him to the ground while he was out for an evening stroll he would have been furious.

'If you don't want people to think you are about to end your life, then don't stand at the very edge of the loch and spread out your arms as if asking God to accept you into heaven.'

'I was enjoying the feel of the rain on my skin,' she said, indignant.

'Good lord,' he murmured. 'English.'

'Excuse me?'

He regarded her for a moment before expanding. 'Only the English would think it a good idea to come walking out in the wilderness in a flimsy cloak and unsuitable boots and then hark on about enjoying the feel of the rain on their skin.'

'And only a brute would attack a woman standing alone at the edge of a lake.'

'I didnae attack you,' he ground out, shaking his head. A moment ago he had resolved to see the young woman back home safely, but now all he could think about was getting away.

Hamish barked, wagging his tail as if enjoying the interaction immensely. He was a working dog, well trained and reliable, but with so much energy even twelve hours running over the Scottish hills could not tire him out. Barking again, he charged forward towards the woman. Callum called out a command

and quick as lightning Hamish obeyed, returning in two bounds to Callum's side, but the young woman had already reacted, taking a step back as she thought Hamish was about to pounce. Her foot landed in a patch of mud and she slithered back, flinging her arms out to the side and a look of horror on her face.

Callum didn't hesitate. If she took one more step back, she would end up in the loch and, even if she could swim, the weight of her clothes would likely drag her down. He did not fancy a dip in the cold water to save her, especially on a night like tonight. He lunged forward and grabbed the front of her dress, grimacing as he heard a rip as the material tore. Quickly he slipped his other arm around her waist. Together they teetered on the edge for a moment, both slipping towards the loch in the mud, and then he managed to pull her back, landing in a pile a few feet away from the water's edge.

This time he was underneath her. She landed in his lap, straddling him, her dress torn at the front. Before he could avert his eyes he caught a glimpse of the soft swell of her breasts and the creamy skin of her chest. Her hips pressed down on to his and if they hadn't been in the mud as the storm raged around them it would have been an erotic position.

Her eyes came up and met him and for a moment

something crackled and pulsed between them. Then Hamish barked, breaking the connection.

With a little gasp of embarrassment she looked down at her torn dress, clutching the ragged edges together to try to protect her modesty. It was pointless, the material was ripped from her neckline to her waist, exposing the white of her chemise underneath.

For a second he thought she might cry, or perhaps accuse him of attacking her again, but instead she surveyed the scene around them, taking in her ripped clothes, their position on the ground and the mud streaked up both their legs. Then she laughed. It started as a bubble of laughter, as if it was something she could not contain, and built and built until there were tears streaming down her cheeks. At first Callum was bemused at her reaction, but the laughter was contagious and he felt his own lips start to twitch.

A minute later she was still straddling him and as she wiped the tears from underneath her eyes she glanced down, seeming only then to realise she hadn't risen and they were still pressed scandalously close together.

'Forgive me,' she murmured, holding his eye and in that moment he wanted nothing more than to reach up and kiss her. Never before had he felt such attraction to a stranger and he wondered if she was one of the mythical creatures of legend the old men told stories of around the fire. Perhaps a selkie, turned human for a night of frolicking out of the water, only to disappear into the waves of the ocean with the sunrise.

'You're forgiven,' he said, his voice soft.

Hamish barked and came to nuzzle against him, no doubt wondering why his master was acting so daft. It was the distraction they both needed and quickly the young woman swung her leg over his body and stood, holding the edges of her ripped dress together. She turned away, taking a moment to adjust her cloak so it covered her bare skin and allowed her to retain a little of her modesty.

'I am sorry for making you so muddy,' she said, her eyes lingering on his body in a way that made him want to snatch her into his arms.

'It will wash out. I hope you will not get into trouble for returning so dishevelled.'

She gave a momentary sad little twitch of her lips, halfway between a smile and a grimace. 'I doubt anyone will notice.'

'There's no protective father or horde of brothers I need to worry about hunting me down for returning you home in such a condition.'

'No,' she said, not elaborating. Normally Callum would leave it at that. He was a man who knew the importance of keeping out of another's business, but the young woman looked so forlorn he wanted to know more.

'Let me escort you home, Miss...'

'Shepherd. Selina Shepherd.'

'I am Callum Thomson. Where are you staying? The inn at Ballachulish?' It was obvious she wasn't local. He was no expert on accents from south of the border, but he did know his Scottish dialects and hers was not one.

She shook her head. 'I'm staying at Loch View Lodge.'

Callum stiffened. He knew Loch View Lodge well, or at least he had when it'd been called Taigh Blath. Ten years ago it had been the heart of his family's lands, the home his ancestors had fought for and ruled from for generations. After his father's death there had been no choice but to sell. It had broken his heart to dispose of the Thomson family legacy and to hand over control of the land and the tenants to some absent Englishman who wished to gather his rents from afar.

He grimaced, regarding Miss Shepherd with a new suspicion. His eyes danced over the plain black cloak and the ripped dress. They were well made, but far from fancy. Clearly she held a decent position in Sir William's party, but he doubted if she was family. Sir William was a wealthy man and he would not have to scrimp and save on fabric and dressmakers for his dependents. Perhaps she was a companion or governess.

'You are with Sir William?' He tried valiantly to keep the disdain from his voice, but from the curious look she gave him he could tell he wasn't successful. She nodded, although did not volunteer any further information.

'You know Sir William?'

'I've never met him, but we have conducted business in the past.' The answer seemed to satisfy her and to his relief he was not pressed to reveal more. He was loath to examine too closely why he didn't want Miss Shepherd to know he was due to meet with Sir William in the morning, to commence negotiations with regards to his daughter's dowry. Callum had no desire to marry a pampered young Miss from London, but it was the price he was going to have to pay to get his land back. 'I will walk with you back to Taigh Blath. The weather is only set to get worse and I do not wish for you to get lost in the hills.'

She hesitated for a moment, but a particularly strong gust of wind whipping at her cloak and the tattered remnants of her dress made her shiver.

'Thank you.'

Chapter Two

At first she struggled to keep up with Mr Thomson's long strides, her boots slipping on the slick grass and her cloak flapping around her legs. The whipping wind and relentless rain did not seem to faze him or the energetic dog that scampered along by his side and she wondered how often they were out in weather such as this.

The sky was dark, heavy with clouds that promised even more rain, and a few times Selina stumbled, her foot catching on some unseen obstacle.

'Here, take my arm,' Mr Thomson said as she almost careened into the back of him. 'The path is uneven.'

'I did not realise we were on a path.'

She glanced at him and saw the hint of a smile. It lit up his face, even though it was present for only a second. He was an attractive man and as she moved closer to take his arm she felt her pulse quicken.

There was something terribly romantic about being caught in a storm with a handsome stranger, especially one who had been so concerned about her welfare.

She slipped her hand into the crook of his elbow and felt him fall into step with her, his pace finally slowing to match her own.

When she had run from the house half an hour earlier, desperate to get away from the suffocating atmosphere and the disdain of her stepmother and half-sister, she had not paid much attention to the route she had taken. Now she realised how fortunate she was that Mr Thomson had approached her by the loch; the house was not visible in the darkness and she had no idea what direction they should be taking.

'It must be fate,' Selina murmured to herself, smiling quickly when Mr Thomson looked down at her. The words had been whipped away by the wind so she was certain he wouldn't have heard her.

'Did you say something?'

'I was just thinking it was fortunate you came along when you did.' She grimaced and looked down, glad the ripped material of her dress was hidden under the fold of her cloak. 'I am not sure I would have been able to find my way back on my own.'

Mr Thomson nodded, his expression serious. 'These hills can be dangerous, even to those of us who spent our childhoods chasing over the countryside. When the mist descends and obscures the natural landmarks it is easy to get turned around.'

'It must have been an idyllic place to grow up. Spending your summers paddling in the loch and winters enjoying the snowfall.'

'Idyllic would not be the right word to describe it,' he said, no hint of humour now on his face. Although their acquaintance had been short she could see how he changed when he spoke about this land that he obviously loved. There was passion in his eyes and sincerity in his words. 'I think this is the most beautiful place in the world. Granted, I have not travelled to every country, but I have seen the vast wildernesses of Canada and the rolling hills of northern England. Nothing compares to the beauty here in the Highlands.'

'You have been to Canada?'

'Aye.'

He did not elaborate, instead ducking his head against a particularly strong gust of wind and pulling Selina forward. Surreptitiously she glanced at him out of the corner of her eye. His manner was not exactly rude, more rough around the edges. It was as if he knew how to interact in polite society, but had not done so for a long time. She felt a surge of anticipation, relishing the challenge that was Mr Callum Thomson.

Before she could start to probe, to use her charm and her conversational skills to break open the shell Mr Thomson had erected around himself, he pointed ahead with his free arm.

'Taigh Blath is just ahead.'

Selina frowned, squinting through the rain. 'Taigh Blath?'

'Loch View Lodge, if you prefer.'

'Taigh Blath is the Scottish translation?'

'No,' he said sharply. 'Taigh Blath is the name of the house. Sir William changed it when he bought the property, although everyone around here still calls it Taigh Blath. A sign on the door does not change the name of a place.' He was holding his body tense and Selina got the impression it wasn't only in an attempt to guard against the weather. She wanted to ask him more about the name, about the history, about the obvious animosity he felt, but already he was pulling away from her.

'Taigh Blath,' she repeated quietly. 'I will remember that.'

'I trust you can make it the rest of the way yourself?'

She hesitated, wondering if he would offer to accompany her to the door if she asked him to, but, sensing his reluctance, she nodded. 'I will slip in the kitchen door.'

Her hand was still in the crook of his elbow and as he stepped away her fingers trailed down his arm, lingering for just a second on his hand. That same jolt she had felt earlier by the loch pulsed through her and for a moment Selina felt as though she could not breathe.

'I wish you well, Miss Shepherd. Don't go wandering at night on your own again.'

Before she could reply he spun and retreated into the darkness, disappearing so quickly that she had the sudden thought that he might be an apparition, shivering before she was able to dismiss the idea and call herself a fool.

Already she missed his solid presence by her side, shielding her from the wind and ensuring she did not lose her footing. He had left her only fifty feet from the back of the house, at the edge of a clear path, but she wished he was still here guiding her.

Quickly she hurried towards the house, repeating the name *'Taigh Blath...'* under her breath again and again, not wanting to forget how lyrical the words had sounded as Mr Thomson had said them. She barely noticed as she reached the door, her mind was too caught up in remembering the way his body had felt underneath hers and the spark that had burned between them as their bodies had collided.

Selina was well aware she had a fanciful imagination and sometimes allowed herself to get caught up in a world filled with things that could never be, but she hadn't imagined the way her body had reacted to Mr Thomson and she was pretty certain she hadn't imagined his response to her either.

'What is the meaning of this?' Lady Kingsley barked as Selina softly closed the door behind her. The kitchen was in darkness and she had thought it deserted, but as her eyes adjusted she saw her stepmother perched on one of the little stools by the kitchen table. She looked out of place and uncomfortable, dressed in the finest fashions London had to offer with her hair pinned immaculately even though they had not entertained guests that evening.

There was always an air of mild desperation about Lady Kingsley. Neither she nor Selina's father had not been born into one of the aristocratic families that ruled London Society. They were both from families of the minor gentry, both desperate to climb higher. Now they could afford the finest clothes and to host extravagant balls, but still they did not quite fit in. It was one of the reasons they were here in Scotland: to secure a marriage with a wealthy and titled suitor for their daughter Catherine. It was just another step towards their goal of being accepted into the highest echelons of Society.

Of course, Selina did not fit into those plans. An illegitimate daughter was not going to help the image Sir William wished to portray. Her father and stepmother had decided to keep her close for now, to limit the chance that she could become an embarrassment, but it did not mean Lady Kingsley had to treat her well.

'I needed some air,' Selina said, hoping the darkness of the kitchen would hide her torn dress.

Lady Kingsley tutted. 'You are a selfish girl. You cannot simply go wandering off without telling anyone where you are.'

'I did not think anyone would notice. I was not gone long.'

'We could have sent people looking for you.'

'Did you?'

There was a pause before Lady Kingsley spoke again. 'That is beside the point. Sir William and I have shown you every courtesy on this trip. The very least you could do is not wander off.'

Even a few weeks ago Selina would have argued with her stepmother. She would have pushed back against her lies and worked herself up until she was in a rage, but now she simply lowered her eyes, murmured an apology she did not mean and silently called Lady Kingsley every name she could think of.

'I will not take up any more of your time,' Selina said, edging towards the door that led to the rest of the house. She clutched the material of her cloak together, feeling a surge of triumph as she escaped from the kitchen without her stepmother noticing the ripped dress. Tomorrow she would have to try to find someone who could help her mend the garment, or if all else failed to dispose of it where no one would see it.

Loch View Lodge was a beautiful house, although not the most logical in design. The oldest part was in the centre, a stone-built building that was more like a fortress than a comfortable residence. The walls were made of heavy blocks of granite and had stood unmoving for centuries. The rest of the house had been added on at various points which led to a charming maze that spread out from the central hall.

The journey to Scotland had felt arduous, even though they had travelled in Sir William's fine carriage. Lady Kingsley grew nauseous if she spent more than an hour in the carriage at a time and it meant frequent stops at the edge of muddy roads. Their progress had been achingly slow and Selina had felt such a relief when they had reached the border and crossed from England to Scotland. She had not realised there were still days of travelling ahead of them.

Throughout the journey they had stayed at reputable inns, but Selina's comfort was not anyone's priority. Sometimes she was assigned to a small truckle bed normally used by a lady's maid so she could be on hand for her mistress. At other times she and Catherine shared a bed and, although the mattress was thicker and the bedding was of better quality, Selina found it difficult to sleep with her spiteful half-sister flailing about in the night and stealing all of the bedsheets.

Once they had arrived in Ballachulish Selina had been surprised to find she was allocated a room to herself. As part of the ruse that she was a distant relative she had been given her own bedchamber. It was small and plainly decorated, but she did not care, it was a space of her own. The grander bedrooms were in the west wing of the house, which had been added on about fifty years earlier, but Selina's room was in the centre, part of the old fortress.

She bowed her head and hurried up the main stairs, hoping she did not see anyone else this evening. All she wanted was to slip out of her sodden clothes, warm herself by the fire in her bedroom and perhaps allow herself to daydream a little about the stoic but handsome Mr Thomson.

'You look terrible,' Catherine said as Selina came round the turn in the staircase. Catherine was twenty-one years old, tall and willowy, with a long face which might have been pretty if she didn't wear such a sour expression all the time. Right now she was perched on a cushioned window seat that was built into a little alcove next to Selina's bedroom. She must have been waiting for Selina, there was no other reason for her to be in this part of the house.

'I was caught in the rain,' Selina said, planning on brushing past Catherine and quickly slipping into her bedroom. It was times like this she missed her sister Sarah acutely. Back home if she ever returned in such a state Sarah would gather her up and insist she sit in the kitchen by the fire while she heated hot water. Only once Selina was warm and dry would she push her to reveal what had happened. Selina felt the tears spring to her eyes, unbidden. She had not seen Sarah for months. Her sister was a faithful correspondent, but with the journey north Selina had not been in one place long enough to send a note with her address, so she could not even console herself with letters.

Shaking her head she thought again what a fool she had been. All this time wasted on her father, a man who clearly did not want anything to do with her, when she could have been spending it with someone who actually cared about her. Her sister was newly married, but Selina did not doubt Sarah would have made space for her in her new life.

'What were you doing in the rain?' Catherine asked, her interest momentarily piqued and then she shook her head as if remembering she did not wish to interact normally with Selina. '*Everyone* knows you do not go wandering around the Scottish countryside at night.'

Selina remained quiet, reaching for her door handle. She'd learned it was best not to engage with Catherine when she was in a combative mood.

Catherine's hand shot out and gripped Selina's shoulder, grasping at the material of her cloak. To Selina's dismay the heavy material parted and revealed the ripped dress underneath, and her exposed chemise and stays.

'Take your hands off me, Catherine,' Selina said, her voice low and tremulous. She pulled the edges of the cloak back together, but it was too late, the state of her clothes had already been revealed. Quickly Selina pushed open her door, thinking she would dart inside and lock it before Catherine could follow. No doubt her half-sister would run straight to her parents to inform them of what Selina had been trying to hide, but Selina found she no longer cared.

Earlier today she had finally decided that she'd had enough. These last few months had been torture, wishing for some connection with her father that she was now realising was never going to materialise. She craved home, the comfort of her sister, the support of her friends. If Sir William thought it best to send her back to England, then she would welcome the decision.

Catherine moved swiftly, following Selina in through her bedroom door before Selina had a chance to close it and turn the key in the lock.

'This is my room, Catherine. Please leave.'

'It's not your room though, is it? This is *my* father's house. He is just letting you stay here for a while.'

'He is my father, too.'

Catherine snorted. 'So you say. No doubt there are a number of candidates who could be your true father.'

Selina had to take a breath to steady herself. Catherine's jibes were not new. In polite society Catherine spoke with tact and grace, but when she and Selina were alone she turned, like a cornered alley cat, becoming vicious.

If she reacted, showed how much the comment about her mother hurt, then Catherine would get a triumphant look on her face and would press harder and harder on the weakness she had just revealed until Selina cracked. It had happened before, especially in the early days when Sir William had reluctantly invited Selina to live with his family, when she had not learned how to control herself around her cruel half-sister.

'What do you want, Catherine?' Selina said instead, trying to act nonchalant as she moved away from the door, all the while fantasising about grabbing the young woman and forcibly propelling her from the room.

At first Catherine did not answer. Instead she wandered around the room, making a critical inspection before sitting down on the bed, rumpling the bedsheets.

'It has been a long evening and I am tired. Either tell me why you were sitting outside my room waiting for me or leave me in peace.'

For a moment Selina thought Catherine was going to press the issue of her ripped dress. She certainly seemed to pause, her eyes flicking over the cloak that was still firmly in place despite the fire that was crackling in the grate, but after a few seconds she lost interest and returned her attention back to her primary reason for being there.

'I don't like you,' Catherine said, her lip curling slightly. 'I don't like you and I don't want you here, but for some unfathomable reason my father thinks it is better to keep you around. Hopefully one day he will regain his sense...'

'Why are you here, Catherine?' Selina asked a little more forcefully.

'Tomorrow I am going to meet the man I am going to marry. You would not understand, but this is what I have been preparing for the last ten years.'

'Since you were eleven years old?'

'The *legitimate* daughters of the titled and wealthy are thinking about marriage as soon as they start to head towards womanhood. Not that I would expect you to know that.'

'What does your impending marriage have to do with me?'

'My future husband is from a long line of Scottish nobility. He will expect things to be done in a certain way and for moral standards to be upheld at all times. Of course, all families have their dirty little secrets, but he will expect discretion.'

'I have no interest in jeopardising your marriage,' Selina said. It was the truth. If Catherine married this Scottish lord she would set up home here in Ballachulish. Selina planned to return first to London and then perhaps to the south coast where she had spent her childhood. You could not get any further from Scotland and that suited her very well indeed.

'Sometimes I can see you think I am unkind towards you, unreasonable in my dislike of you,' Catherine said, her eyes boring into Selina. 'But understand this. If you do even the tiniest little thing that could upset my future husband, I will not rest until I have destroyed you.'

Selina sighed, suddenly feeling very weary. 'You have my word that I will be as absent as possible and, when my presence is required, I will do nothing scandalous, nothing to draw attention to myself. I doubt your future husband will even know I am there.'

Catherine looked a little mollified and to Selina's relief she rose from the bed, brushing past Selina on her way to the door. Before she left the room she paused, looking back over her shoulder.

'You never know, perhaps he has a stableboy or gardener who might stoop to marry you.'

She was gone before Selina could respond, gliding away down the corridor as if she was on her way to meet the Queen.

Only once the door was shut and locked did Selina begin to relax. She peeled off the sodden cloak, revealing the extent of the damage done to her dress. Grimacing, she carefully stripped off the ripped garment and laid it over a chair. She would look at it with fresh eyes in the morning, but it did not look to be salvageable.

What she wanted right now was a warm basin of water, or even better a steaming bath in front of the fire, but to ring for the servants to heat water at this time of night would only invite further scrutiny from her stepmother.

Once she had undressed to her chemise she moved closer to the fire, screwing up her nose as the wet hem of the thin cotton undergarment brushed against her legs. Ensuring the curtains were tightly pulled and the door locked, she gripped the hem of the chemise and lifted it over her head.

The fire in the grate warmed her skin and, after a few minutes, she felt more like herself and less like a drowned rat. She crossed her arms over her body and ran her fingers over the soft skin of her shoulders, enjoying the caress. She missed being touched, not that anyone had ever touched her in a romantic way, but she missed the heartfelt embraces from her sister and her mother, she missed the way her friends would take her by the hand as they strolled along the promenade in St Leonards.

Her thoughts skipped to the man she had met tonight and for a moment she wondered what it would feel like to have his fingers caressing her skin. His hands had been rough and he was undoubtably strong, but she imagined him as gentle when he touched her.

She took a shuddering breath in and stepped away from the fire. Always she had been prone to indulging in wild flights of imagination. She would get caught up in an idea and allow her thoughts to run away from her. Selina was not stupid, she was aware of what was realistic in her life and what was not, but often she drifted off into fantasy anyway. It was what had got her into this mess with her father. Most people would accept that the man wanted nothing to do with the daughters he had abandoned before their birth, but Selina had pursued the dream that he would one day welcome her into his family and secure for her a happy future.

'You are an air-headed fool, Selina Shepherd,' she murmured, stalking over to the bed and pulling on her nightclothes.

Tomorrow she would begin planning how to escape from the mess she had got herself into and return to England as soon as possible.

Chapter Three

'Stay,' Callum instructed Hamish as they paused outside the front door of Taigh Blath. Hamish was a working dog, trained to follow commands in an instant, and as soon as the word was out of Callum's mouth Hamish stopped, sitting down in the shade of the house. 'I wish I could take you in with me, boy,' Callum muttered. 'But you don't want to be subjected to this torture.'

From the outside the house looked unchanged. In the years since he had sold the land and property to Sir William the new owner had only visited a handful of times. Normally a local couple were left in charge, airing out the rooms periodically and keeping everything ticking over. It was a travesty for such a beautiful place to be locked up for most of the year. It was meant to be a home, not merely a symbol of wealth.

He raised his hand and knocked on the door, surprised to see it opened immediately by a footman dressed in a smart livery, his hair slicked back from his face.

'Lord Leven,' he said. The footman waited a second, looking at his hand expectantly, and Callum realised he was expecting a card. He'd never understand the idiosyncrasies of London Society and he never felt the desire to either.

After a moment, when a card was not forthcoming, the footman gave an embarrassed little bow and led the way into the house.

Callum moved over the threshold, trying to ignore the squeeze in his chest as he stepped into the house that had once been his birthright. There were good memories here, along with the bad. For every night he had heard his father stumbling around in a drunken haze, throwing glasses at the servants, there had been another where his mother would sneak him down from his bed in the nursery to take him walking in the moonlight. For a moment he felt as though the memories might overwhelm him, but with great effort he pushed them away. Today was about the future, not the past.

'Good afternoon,' he said as he entered the drawing room. The scene before him looked staged and he wondered if people really did spend their time posed in such a way. Sir William was standing by the window, his stance wide and hands clasped behind his back, looking every bit the master of everything he surveyed. Lady Kingsley was perched in a straight-backed chair, a square of embroidery laying on her lap. In the centre of the tableau was Miss Catherine Kingsley, the young woman he had come here to meet. The young woman he was set to marry despite today being the first time he laid eyes on her.

The ladies rose and Sir William turned, striding over to clasp Callum by the hand, squeezing and shaking firmly.

'Lord Leven, a pleasure to meet you, a real pleasure.'

'And you, Sir William.'

'This is my lovely wife, Lady Kingsley, and my daughter, Miss Catherine Kingsley.'

Callum bowed to them each in turn, feeling ridiculously formal.

'Please have a seat, we are eager to get to know you, Lord Leven,' Lady Kingsley said, beaming at him.

The obvious spot for him to take was the one right next to Miss Kingsley. All three Kingsleys were looking at it, directing him there with his eyes. While Callum did not like to be manipulated, this wasn't a battle that was worth fighting.

Today had been arranged so he could meet Miss Kingsley. The negotiations had partly taken place over a lengthy correspondence between himself and Sir William and they would conclude in the coming days in private, but today was purely for both him and the Kingsleys to ensure there was nothing so terrible about the other that it would stop the deal that had been worked on for so long.

He sat, his large form feeling out of place on the dainty seat. The furniture was new, although Callum was not surprised. When he had sold the house to Sir William the contents had been sold alongside it. Everything was sturdy and well made, and no doubt in the less public areas the old furniture had been retained, but the drawing room was the public face of the house. It would be the first area to be updated. Despite his mother's best efforts his father had lost interest in entertaining not long after they were married. The drawing room had not been used for its true purpose for a long time before Sir William had taken over the place.

The silence stretched out, long and uncomfortable, before Lady Kingsley and Miss Kingsley rushed to fill it at the same time.

'My daughter is most accomplished at her needlework, my lord,' Lady Kingsley said, motioning to the square of fabric in the young woman's hands.

Callum knew nothing whatsoever about needlework, at least not this sort which seemed to be about sewing pretty flowers on a piece of fabric. He'd mended his own clothes before, pulling a blunt needle through frayed material in times of necessity, his endeavours always ending up looking rudimentary.

Once he had even stitched his own skin after sustaining a deep cut in the wilds of Canada. He'd been three days from any sort of civilisation and the injury was deep and gushing blood. The only way to stop it was to sew the edges together. He now sported a ragged scar on his left leg, but he didn't think Miss Kingsley would appreciate hearing about this.

'Very accomplished,' he murmured.

'It is such a pleasant day, perhaps we could go for a stroll in the gardens,' Miss Kingsley said, bestowing him with a little smile.

He inclined his head, suddenly eager to get out of the room.

'A wonderful idea,' Lady Kingsley said, clapping her hands.

As they stepped out through the doors that led on to a terrace at the back of the house Callum found himself looking around to see if he could spot the woman he had met the night before by the lake. Despite only spending a few minutes in her company she had plagued his thoughts the evening before, distracting him when he was meant to be preparing for this meeting.

'I am glad we are to spend a few minutes alone,' Miss Kingsley said, looking up at him with an expression of innocent infatuation. She was young, although not in the first flush of youth and must have been out in Society for a few years, and he sensed an air of calculation about her. The innocent expression seemed curated, as did her every gesture, her every move. Callum became even more convinced of this when her arm accidentally brushed against his and she let out a little gasp.

'I am glad of it, too,' he said, trying to release some of the tension he was holding in his shoulders. 'The gardens are looking lovely.'

His companion glanced at the neat borders of flowers without much interest and then turned back to him. Callum allowed his gaze to linger. *This* was why he was going through with a marriage to a stranger. It would all be worth it when he regained control of his ancestral home. His eyes rested on the shimmer of the loch in the distance and rise of the hills beyond. It was beautiful.

With his reasons for doing this refocused, he reluctantly pulled his eyes away from the view and regarded Miss Kingsley. She was tall and slender with an expensive dress that had been carefully tailored to show off her best attributes. Certainly there didn't seem to be anything wrong with the young woman, although he did not feel anything except mild resentment towards her.

'Tell me about yourself,' he said.

'Oh, where to begin?' She hesitated just a moment before launching into a list of her attributes. 'I'm a simple girl really. I love the whirl of Society and some say I am the finest dancer at our local balls, but I also enjoy the comfort and stability of a good home life. I am excellent at keeping domestic staff in order and my mother has taught me to run a tight, disciplined household. Once I am married I look forward to being a good wife and mother.' She glanced at him with momentary panic in her eyes as if she realised she might be scaring him off. 'When the time is right, of course.'

'Of course,' he murmured. He wanted children, although at the moment the idea of them seemed like an abstract thought rather than something he could really picture. He had been an only child, unusual among his peers. The boys he had grown up with had all been from large, boisterous families and when he had been younger he'd yearned for that.

'How about you, my lord? What is it you enjoy?'

Callum cleared his throat, wondering if this would get easier. They were from different worlds, he and Miss Kingsley, and right now he could not imagine a time when they would be comfortable in one another's company. He didn't have vast estates and multiple homes to allow him and his wife to lead separate lives. They would be together from the very start. The idea made Callum uncomfortable. For so long it had been just him and Hamish. He wasn't sure he would be very good at sharing his space with someone else.

'I enjoy my work, Miss Kingsley, and spending time outside. I like walking in the hills and taking a rowboat out on the loch.'

Miss Kingsley sniffed, looking out into the distance at the hills he was talking about, a frown on her face as if she could not understand his enjoyment of the local scenery.

They had reached the edge of the small formal garden that was laid out to match the width of the house. It had been his mother's pride and joy and he was pleased to see some of her favourite flowers still flourishing.

Before he could ask Miss Kingsley any more mundane questions he heard Hamish start to bark at the front of the house. As a general rule Hamish was a well-behaved dog. Callum had rescued him as a pup while he was in Canada and they had been inseparable since. Trained in some of the most severe conditions possible, used to freezing temperatures and some days with only meagre rations, Hamish was a working dog first and foremost, but as the years had passed Callum had softened some of his rules and now the hunting dog was more pet than working animal.

Normally if told to sit and wait, Hamish would find a quiet spot and wait patiently for Callum's return. It was unusual to hear him bark like this and Callum immediately was on alert.

'Please excuse me for a moment,' he said, giving her a quick, reassuring smile and then striding off down the side of the house. Part of him wondered if this was an unnecessary distraction, a way for him to dodge the reality of his future for just a few more minutes. As he rounded the front of the house he stopped abruptly and Miss Kingsley, who had followed him rather than wait for him in the gardens, barrelled into the back of him. Absently he reached out an arm to steady her, but his eyes were fixed on the scene in front of him.

'Miss Shepherd, I must insist you put my dog down.'

The young woman he had met the night before turned to him, cradling Hamish as though he was a lapdog, not a serious, working animal, and smiled at him for just a second. The smile pierced right through Callum's chest and for a moment he felt as though he couldn't breathe. Almost immediately Miss Shepherd's eyes flicked over his shoulder and the warmth drained from her, her whole body stiffening.

'What are you doing, Selina?' Miss Kingsley snapped, her voice clipped and the irritation obvious in her tone. 'You were meant to be upstairs.'

'I came out for some air.'

'How do you two know one another?' Miss Kingsley said. Gone was the charming smile and smooth voice she had been using when it was just the two of them.

Miss Shepherd flashed him a look of desperation.

'We don't,' Callum said, turning to his future fiancée. 'I live nearby and I met Miss Shepherd when we were both out walking.'

'You didn't mention it,' Miss Kingsley said, her eyes still on Miss Shepherd. There was definitely an animosity there and he didn't like how Miss Shepherd shrank back under Miss Kingsley's scrutiny. Most of his childhood lessons had come from his mother rather than his father and one of her favourites had been that you could tell a lot about a person by the way they treated the people below them. He wasn't sure if Miss Shepherd was some sort of paid companion or governess, but she was clearly inferior in the hierarchy of this family to Miss Kingsley, and the daughter of the family was not treating her kindly.

'I did not realise the significance,' Miss Shepherd

said, regaining a little of her colour. 'I was not aware Mr Thomson was the gentleman due to call on you today.'

For a long moment Miss Kingsley eyed Miss Shepherd with suspicion and then seemed to remember Callum was there.

'*Lord* Leven,' Miss Kingsley corrected her. 'Put down poor Lord Leven's dog, Selina. Then I expect you have some letters to write in your room. We would hate to keep you away from your important correspondence.'

Slowly Miss Shepherd lowered Hamish to the floor. He let out a whine of disappointment and then jumped up to lick Miss Shepherd's hand as she straightened.

'You have made a friend, Miss Shepherd. Hamish isn't usually this easily enamoured with people.'

For a second their eyes met and Callum felt the air pulse and crackle between them. It was a feeling unlike anything he had ever felt before and he had to force himself to turn away.

'Hamish is a lovely dog, although unusual.'

'I doubt you are an expert on dog breeds,' Miss Kingsley said before turning back to Callum and laying a hand on his arm. He had to resist the urge to shrug it off. Instead he reminded himself why he was doing all of this and smiled at his future fiancée.

'There you are,' Lady Kingsley said, appearing

from the back of the house on the path he and Miss Kingsley had taken a few seconds earlier. 'I was worried when you disappeared from view. I know we will soon be family, Lord Leven, but a mother still has to protect her daughter's reputation.' Lady Kingsley paused, taking a moment to survey the scene in front of her. 'Should you not be inside, Miss Shepherd?'

He could see how hard it was for Miss Shepherd to summon a bland smile and incline her head towards the older woman.

'Good day, Lord Leven. I hope you enjoy your visit to Taigh Blath.'

She turned and before he could think better of it, he had stepped forward, wanting to prolong their interaction. Quickly he caught himself. He was not here to indulge his whims, he was here to secure the future of his people and his family's legacy.

'Good day,' he said quietly as she walked inside.

Chapter Four

After thirty minutes of pacing in her room Selina felt as though she were going mad. She needed fresh air and the wind on her face. What she really wanted was a bracing sea breeze and a walk along the cliffs arm in arm with her sister in their home town, but St Leonards-on-Sea was over five hundred miles away. It might as well be on the other side of the world.

She glanced out the window, noting the gardens were deserted, and decided to risk her stepmother and half-sister's wrath by slipping out. It was unlikely they would catch her again, not while they were occupied with Lord Leven in the drawing room or wherever they had disappeared to once she had been banished upstairs.

Selina felt a swell of frustration at the thought of Catherine sitting there, pretending to be a young woman of good character. It wasn't her place to warn Lord Leven what a horrible family he was marrying into. He was a grown man, capable of making his own assessments and decisions, and she was aware there were many reasons for the match. It was not as if he had been conned into a false love match. No doubt his reasons for wanting to marry Catherine were as mercenary as Sir William's.

Her cloak was still a little damp around the hem from the night before, but she had no other outer layer to keep her warm, and she was fast learning how quickly the weather could change here in the Highlands. It would be warm and sunny one minute and the next the clouds and mist would roll in and drop the temperature by ten degrees.

Thankfully the hall was deserted and she made it outside without anyone spotting her. Hamish, Lord Leven's dog, was gone from his position keeping guard by the front door and Selina wondered if that meant Lord Leven had left already, or if the dog had been taken elsewhere. There was a sizeable stable yard here at Loch View Lodge and she would not put it past her stepmother to have instructed one of the grooms to move the animal somewhere she deemed more suitable.

Selina walked quickly, not wanting anyone from the house to see her. After the storm the night before the sky was clear and the sun shining. There was a warmth in the air that Selina had not felt since crossing the border, although when the breeze blew there was a little chill.

As soon as she could she left the main drive, cutting across the grass and looping around the edge of the property towards the loch. It was difficult to tell where the edge of the estate that belonged to Loch View Lodge was for there was no fence, no marker of boundary, just a continuation of the rolling countryside.

In the daylight it was much easier to stick to a path of sorts and as she came out into sunshine from a dense patch of trees in the distance she could even see the village of Ballachulish. As she walked she felt some of the tension in her body begin to melt away. There was nothing like fresh air and gentle exercise to clear the mind.

It had taken her fifteen minutes to reach the water's edge and by the time she arrived she felt much better about everything. She had resolved to forget about Lord Leven and Catherine, to wish them well in their union and focus on planning her escape back to England, back home. *That* was what was important.

A tall alder tree sat at the water's edge, angled back away from the water like an old man leaning on his stick. It had a few branches at shoulder height and

Selina could not resist the urge to see if there was a way to pull herself up.

It was an easy enough climb and within a minute she was sitting with her back against the trunk of the tree, her legs stretched out along the thick branch. It was a comfortable seat and a beautiful spot, with a view along the vast length of the loch in front of her.

Despite her desire to flee Scotland and return home, Selina had to admit she was grateful she had had the opportunity to travel somewhere so beautiful. Not many people ever got the chance to leave their home town, let alone spend weeks on the road to end up somewhere so far away.

As thoughts of Scotland and thoughts of home mingled she felt her eyes drooping. The sun on her face and the disturbed night she'd spent tossing and turning in bed meant she felt drowsy and, after ensuring she was secure in her seat, she closed her eyes and allowed the fatigue to overtake her.

She awoke to the horrible sensation of falling. In her dream she had been teetering on the edge of a cliff, looking at the crashing waves below, and the cliff had started to crumble under her feet.

Selina's eyes shot open and for a moment she did not understand what was happening or where she was.

'Damn it, woman, grab on.' Lord Leven's gruff

voice came from somewhere below her. In her drowsy state she became aware of the pressure on her hip and after a moment of confusion she realised where she was.

Below her Lord Leven was standing, his arms raised and his hands pushing against her hip and her thigh. The force he was applying was the only thing stopping her from falling the five feet from the tree to the ground.

Selina's arms shot out and she gripped hold of the branch, steadying herself and managing to reposition herself so she was no longer off balance. Lord Leven waited for a few seconds longer until he let go, no doubt not trusting her not to fall on top of him.

Once her heart had slowed in her chest she looked down to find Lord Leven glaring up at her.

'What sort of fool decides to sleep in a tree?' He shook his head in disbelief. 'The comfortable beds at Taigh Blath not good enough for you?'

Selina bristled even though she knew he had a point. Allowing herself to drift off to sleep on a tree branch, however safe and sturdy it had felt, had been a foolish move.

'It is not that far to the ground,' Selina said, glancing down and trying to disguise a grimace. 'You could have let me fall if it irked you so much to assist me.'

'A broken leg is no minor inconvenience, Miss Shepherd. That sort of injury can ruin a person's life.' He spoke with an authority that convinced Selina he had seen an injury such as that before.

She hesitated for a second and then gave a little nod. 'Thank you for your assistance.'

'What are you doing up there?'

'It is a comfortable perch with an excellent view and with the sun on my face I closed my eyes for a moment and drifted off to sleep.' She cocked her head to the side. 'Should you not be in Sir William's drawing room, rather than out here saving me from self-inflicted injuries?'

'Ah. Aye. Most likely.'

'It did not go well?'

He did not answer the question, but instead gave her a searching look.

'What is your connection to the family, Miss Shepherd?'

'You want to check I am not Miss Kingsley's treasured childhood friend before you vent your frustrations?'

'Are you? She did not treat you as such.'

'No. I am…' Selina hesitated, having to resist the urge to tell Lord Leven the truth. 'A very distant, very poor relative of Sir William. Sir William and

Lady Kingsley were kind enough to bring me along on this trip to act as companion to Miss Kingsley.'

'The same Miss Kingsley who hates you?'

Selina spluttered. 'She said she hated me?'

'No, she did her very best to pretend you dinnae exist, but she wasn't exactly pleasant to you when we met outside Taigh Blath.'

'We do not share many interests,' Selina said carefully. That was a lie. Initially Selina had wondered if she and Catherine might one day become friends, for they both enjoyed socialising and fashion, but Catherine had refused to ever speak to Selina about anything at all. The only time they interacted was for Catherine to bark an order or voice her disdain in some way.

To her surprise Lord Leven motioned for her to shuffle up and then pulled himself on to the branch beside her. She moved along a little, but when he joined her his legs brushed against hers.

'It is quite a view up here,' he said, nodding out at the loch.

'It is. And this is a comfortable branch.'

'You'll not convince me it is a sensible place to take a nap, Miss Shepherd.' He glanced at her and smiled. There was something charming underneath the gruff exterior, as if Lord Leven was a man of two halves, perhaps even bridging two worlds. There was the gentleman, refined and polite, and then the rougher, more direct man who looked uncomfortable in the cravat he had been forced to wear.

'Did you accomplish everything that you needed to with Sir William and Miss Kingsley?' Selina wasn't sure why she was quite so bothered about this marriage. She barely knew Lord Leven. One brief interaction and a night of fantasising did not mean she had any claim on him, yet she felt inordinately upset that he was the one who would be marrying Catherine.

'No.' He didn't look at her, instead locked his eyes on the horizon, a pensive expression on his face. 'It seems the negotiations are to be more complicated than I first anticipated.'

'Sir William is being difficult?'

'Aye, I should have expected as much. He has a reputation as a canny man in business, I dinnae ken why I thought this would be any different.'

'It is just a business deal, then?'

'What else is a marriage?'

'That is a cynical view of the world.'

'Not all of us have the luxury of romance.'

They fell silent and Selina realised Lord Leven was troubled by his impending engagement.

'I understand there are many reasons for people to get married. I am not so naive to think everyone can be blessed with a marriage built on a foundation of love. Yet surely if you are committing to someone for the rest of your life it is important to at least value what they bring to the partnership other than money or status.'

'I do not know Miss Kingsley. We have spent but a few minutes in one another's company and throughout that time it felt as though I was not seeing her true character.'

Selina bit down a remark about Catherine's true character. She did not want to scare Lord Leven off.

'But you will get to spend more time with her before you marry?'

'Aye, a little.' He shrugged. 'I do not wish to shatter your romantic expectations, Miss Shepherd, but I would marry Miss Kingsley even if she was responsible for every atrocity ever committed, even if she was the worst person to walk this earth.'

Selina laughed, thinking he was joking, cutting the sound short when she realised he was completely serious.

'You must really want what Sir William has to offer.' She wanted to ask him what it was he wanted from Sir William, what was so important that he would consent to marry a stranger, no matter how much he liked or disliked her. Selina was about to ask more when she heard a faint voice in the distance, calling her name.

'It seems you are missed,' Lord Leven said, moving to hop down from the tree.

The voice was getting a little louder, the sound carried on the light breeze.

'I suppose there is a first time for everything.' Selina shuffled along the branch, suddenly aware how inappropriate it was to be sitting here with her half-sister's future husband. They were alone, unchaperoned, and to a suspicious mind anything could have happened between them. 'Catherine cannot see us together.'

Lord Leven looked up at her and reached out a hand, giving her a wink that set her pulse racing. 'I've been roaming these hills and glens since I could first walk, I can disappear in an instant.'

Selina braced herself against the branch, getting ready to push off, to launch herself into the air. As she leaned forward she felt her dress snag against something and she pulled back, but not enough. She was off balance, desperate not to ruin another dress, her arms flailing as she grabbed for something to steady herself on.

She slipped forward and as she started to fall she wondered if she might end up with a broken leg after all.

Strong hands gripped her hips, holding her suspended for a moment before slowly lowering her to the ground. It was a show of strength like nothing Selina had seen before and she realised quite how powerful Lord Leven was, to be able to arrest her fall in mid-air and then control her descent to the ground.

As he lowered her, her body slid down his. It was unavoidable, but Selina felt her breath catch in her chest as her lips passed mere inches from his. Even when her feet touched the ground she was unable to move, unable to step away.

Her chin was tilted up, her eyes fixed on his, and in that moment Selina wanted nothing more than for him to kiss her. She thought she could see desire in his eyes, that flare of attraction, but if it was ever there at all it was quickly hidden.

In the space of just a few seconds Selina's thoughts spiralled. She imagined him kissing her, running his fingers along her cheek. She imagined them standing together hand in hand at the edge of the loch and then in a church and then…

Taking a deep, shuddering breath, she turned and stepped away. Her runaway imagination and willingness to indulge it had got her into this predicament she found herself in—far from home with people who hated her and no real prospects for the future. She would not fall down another rabbit hole of self-indulgence, fantasising about this man who had just told her he would stop at nothing to marry her half-sister.

'Thank you again, Lord Leven,' she said, surprised to hear her voice calm and steady.

'Until tonight, Miss Shepherd.'

Behind them Catherine called out again, this time much closer. Selina turned in panic to see her half-sister come into view and readied herself for the anger that would spew from Catherine when she realised Selina had been fraternising with Lord Leven.

'Where on earth have you been? Mother is beside herself with irritation. She says you are never where you are meant to be and she's right, it is annoying.'

Selina blinked, surprised at the tone of Catherine's voice. Her stepsister might only be twenty-one, but she knew better than to talk to Selina in that way in front of others, especially the man she was hoping to marry.

'Why are you standing there, gawping like an ugly fish?'

Looking over her shoulder, Selina was surprised to find Lord Leven had disappeared. She was standing on her own under the tree with no sign of him or Hamish. He had slipped away silently, as promised, like a hero from ancient myth.

Chapter Five

With one last, unhappy, tug on his cravat Callum knocked at the door. It felt odd to stand outside his own home, to knock on the door and have to wait to be invited in, but he was not a man who had always taken the easy path through life and he knew with a certainty that burned bright inside him that one day Taigh Blath would be his again.

The door opened and he was ushered inside. He was greeted by the dulcet sounds of a piano and Lady Kingsley hurrying down the stairs to meet him.

'Lord Leven, a pleasure to see you again. We are lucky to have you as our guest twice in one day.'

She brushed a hand lightly along his back and ushered him towards the drawing room and the sound of the piano.

'My daughter will be down momentarily. She wanted to look her very best for you,' Lady Kingsley said as she showed him to a seat and clicked her fingers at a footman who appeared at her side in an instant carrying a tray of drinks. 'Champagne. We will soon be celebrating after all.'

'Thank you.' He took the glass and raised it to his lips to take a fortifying gulp. It would be good to have something to settle his nerves. There were a lot of people relying on him getting this right, a lot of people who would be keen to see the back of the Kingsleys for good if he could negotiate the return of some of his ancestral lands.

'I will let Catherine know you have arrived and hurry her along.'

Lady Kingsley glided over to the piano and leaned down, murmuring something he couldn't quite catch before leaving the room. From his position he could only see the top of the head of the young woman playing the piano, but even from just a few strands of hair he knew it was Miss Shepherd. She played well, her fingers dancing easily over the keys and the music clear and well paced.

Callum thought back to their encounter earlier that afternoon, the time they had spent sitting on the tree branch together, and inevitably his mind jumped to the moment he had helped her from the branch. His hands had grabbed her hips and as he'd lowered her to the ground she had slid down his body. It had been an intimate moment and one that he could not stop thinking about. Normally he prided himself on being someone who was fully in control of his actions and emotions, but in that moment if she had lingered a second longer he would have kissed her.

Kissed her and jeopardised everything he had been working for these last ten years.

The sensible thing to do now would be to sit in his chair and sip his champagne while waiting for the Kingsley family to appear.

Callum tapped his fingers on the arm of the chair, straining his neck to catch a glimpse of Miss Shepherd's face. She had not missed a single note since he had entered the house, not even when Lady Kingsley went to speak with her. He shifted in his chair, telling himself to stay put, but the urge to move got too much and before he could stop himself he was on his feet and halfway to the piano.

'You play well,' he said, coming to stand behind Miss Shepherd's left shoulder.

'I play adequately. I can follow the music, match the desired melody and tempo.'

'You speak as though that is not a skill.'

'If you heard my sister play, you would understand what a talented pianist was. When her fingers touch the keys it is as if she becomes one with the music. Every note is infused with meaning and sentiment.' Miss Shepherd spoke without turning, her eyes following the music, but it was obvious she only needed to utilise a little of her brain to play the familiar piece.

'Your sister is not here with you in Scotland?'

'No. She was recently married.'

Miss Shepherd flicked her head subtly and Callum saw a stray strand of hair that had come loose from the pins that must be tickling her neck. Without thinking he reached out and hooked the curled strand with his index finger, moving it back over her shoulder to where it would not irritate her. As he did so she leaned ever so slightly towards him and his fingers brushed against her neck. She stiffened and missed the next note, the silence emphasising how inappropriate his touch had been.

'Forgive me,' he murmured.

'You should sit down, my lord. My...' She paused, correcting herself. 'Lady Kingsley will not be happy if she sees me talking to you.'

'Why not?'

'It is not my place.'

'That is what she said to you?'

Miss Shepherd sighed. 'Why does it bother you? You do not know me.'

She was right, of course. The sensible thing to do would be to walk back over to his chair and sit sipping his champagne while he waited for his future fiancée and her parents to be ready for the evening ahead.

Callum did not move. His feet were planted firmly and he doubted even the strongest of men could have shifted him in that instant.

'I do not wish to get you into trouble...'

'Sit down, then.'

'Thankfully, most of my traits and behaviours I get from my mother, but my obstinance, my dislike of being manipulated, that is a trait my father possessed.'

'I'm not manipulating you.'

'I know. Lady Kingsley, on the other hand, strikes me as someone who prides herself in being a puppeteer.'

This earned him an assessing glance, although only a momentary one. Miss Shepherd had regained her composure and she wasn't going to be easily distracted again.

'Lady Kingsley reminded me of my place,' Miss Shepherd said eventually.

'What *is* your place?'

'I told you. Distant relative, unwanted companion, someone who certainly should not do anything to jeopardise the marriage negotiations the Kingsley family have travelled four hundred miles to complete.'

'Move over,' Callum said, tapping her lightly on the shoulder when she stayed right where she was.

'Return to your seat, my lord.'

'The next part is played best as a duet.'

Miss Shepherd scoffed. 'It sounds perfectly fine played alone.'

'It sounds better with two. Move over or I will have to sit on you.'

This got her moving, shifting along the piano stool as if one end was on fire. Callum sat down next to her, wondering why he was persisting in bothering her rather than sitting in the comfortable chair at the other end of the drawing room.

Part of him wondered if it was his mind's subtle way of trying to sabotage this arrangement with the Kingsleys. On the whole he did not oppose the idea of marriage, but never had he wanted to marry a complete stranger, especially one who was used to a vastly different life to the one he could offer.

He was no fool—the Kingsleys were obscenely wealthy and what Sir William coveted was a link to the aristocracy. No one in England had agreed to tie themselves to the social climbing family, so Sir William had started to look further afield. Miss Kingsley would become Lady Leven, Countess of Leven when they married, but she would not live in the luxury she had grown used to. It could make for an unhappy marriage.

Despite all this he was resolved to go through with the match. Too many people were relying on him for him to back out now, but despite this resolution he was aware of his own reluctance and wondered if this sudden desire for Miss Shepherd was a symptom of that.

Pushing the thought away, he concentrated on the music, his fingers dancing over the keys, playing the lower notes in accompaniment to her higher ones. He kept his eyes trained on the piano, aware he had not played for a very long time, but he felt Miss Shepherd glance at him once or twice and felt the curiosity in her look.

He played the last notes with a flourish and neither of them moved as the sound faded away.

'I didn't imagine you could play the piano,' Miss Shepherd said quietly.

'You have been thinking about me, then?'

Colour flooded to Miss Shepherd's cheeks and he felt something tighten and pulse inside him as she bit her lip. Callum was a man of the world. Despite dedicating the last decade of his life to rebuilding some of the fortune his father had lost, he had on occasion taken time to appreciate worldly pleasures. There had been no woman who he had felt the urge to settle down with, but he'd had dalliances. He recognised the flare of desire and knew he had to quickly distance himself before he ruined everything.

Clearing his throat he stood, stepping away just in time as footsteps became audible from the stairs. After a few seconds Miss Kingsley burst into the room in a haze of perfume. She was dressed in a gown made from the finest pale-blue silk with a thousand tiny white flowers embroidered on the fabric. It seemed out of place here in a drawing room in the Highlands, but they were clearly trying to impress him with their show of wealth. Callum consoled himself that it was reassuring they were doing so much to entice him; despite the slow start the negotiations must mean as much to the Kingsleys as they did to him.

Miss Kingsley flashed a quick glare at Miss Shepherd, quickly covering the expression as she turned to face him, her lips spread into a beatific smile.

'Lord Leven, I am sorry to keep you waiting. I wanted to look my very best for you.' She gave a pretty little curtsy and looked up at him from under lowered lashes. Callum was not so starved of polite society that he didn't know now was when he was meant to offer a compliment.

'You look very...nice,' he ventured.

'And you look dashing,' Miss Kingsley said, stepping forward to lay a hand on his arm. 'I am just sorry I was not here to receive you.'

'Miss Shepherd was kind enough to keep me company.' As soon as the words were out of his mouth he realised he'd made a mistake. The atmosphere in the room turned instantaneously frosty.

'Wonderful,' Lady Kingsley said after a moment, ushering Callum to a seat, her expression stony. 'Miss Shepherd is a comfort to us all.'

There was a pause as everyone sat, Miss Kingsley taking up a perch next to him, her legs angled towards him. He was struck again by how young she looked, although by her behaviour you would not know it. Someone had taught her all the wiles a young woman was meant to employ while trying to ensnare a husband, but it looked as though his was her first try at using them. Everything felt a bit awkward, a bit forced.

'Selina, join us,' Sir William called over his shoulder. Miss Shepherd hesitated, looking surprised at the invitation, but obediently she came and sat with them. 'I wonder, Lord Leven, you know all about our family, but we do not know about yours. Do you have many relatives living close by?'

'The Thomson clan is not as big as it once was, but there are still quite a few of us in the area.' He didn't like talking about his family, not with outsiders. There was a long history of misery and woe that had led the once-powerful Thomsons to the position they were in now. Many had left the area, travelling south to try their luck in the burgeoning cities in northern England, or like him had taken a ship further afield to Canada or the United States. The people who had stayed were those who had found it harder to start a new life elsewhere. The old and infirm, or those with lots of young children.

'Your family have held land in the area for centuries, I believe?' Sir William said.

'We have.' He thought of the small parcel of land with two small cottages on it—that was all that was left now. It had been the worst moment of his life, that moment he'd had to sell Taigh Blath and all the estate land that went with it.

'It must be nice, having somewhere you feel a deep connection to,' Miss Shepherd said quietly, her cheeks flushing as all eyes turned to her. 'To know your ancestors walked the same paths, fished in the same lochs, climbed the same trees.'

'I hardly think Lord Leven spends his time climbing trees,' Miss Kingsley snorted. 'He is an earl, not one of the fishermen you grew up with.'

Callum's eyes widened a little at the venom in Miss Kingsley's voice. Turning to Miss Shepherd, he smiled softly, trying to reassure her. 'This land is a part of me as much as any flesh or blood. I know every path, every hill, every single inch of it. I know where the soil is fertile and perfect for crops and where the ground holds too much water and if you plant any seeds they will rot before they can sprout.'

'You learned this as a child?'

'Yes. Not from my father, he was not a careful caretaker of Taigh Blath and the estate, but from other members of my family.'

'Selina, you overstep,' Miss Kingsley said sharply. 'Can you not see you have upset our guest, talking of the past.'

Miss Shepherd pressed her lips together in a way that made Callum suspect she was biting down a scathing retort and not for the first time he wondered what her true relationship was with the Kingsley family. None of them seemed particularly kind to her. Miss Kingsley was unable to hide her dislike and Lady Kingsley was not much better. Sir William seemed less openly antagonistic, but he wasn't exactly warm to the young woman.

Thankfully the awkwardness was cut short by a footman entering the room to announce dinner.

As he stood Miss Kingsley gripped hold of his arm, smiling up at him. He had to suppress a shudder, telling himself there was nothing wrong with the young woman. She was keen, that was all, and given his reluctance he found her attitude a little too much, but he would have to get over it.

'My dear, would you show Lord Leven into the dining room. I wish to have a word with Catherine and Selina. We will be no more than a minute.' Sir William spoke directly to his wife, motioning for her and their guest to go on ahead.

Lady Kingsley looked thrown, but like a consummate hostess she just smiled and nodded, guiding Callum from the room into another opulent setting. Callum strained to hear what was being said in the drawing room, but the walls were too thick and Sir William's voice too low.

Chapter Six

'She is ruining everything,' Catherine said with a pout. It was all Selina could do to stop rolling her eyes.

'He likes her,' Sir William said, nodding his head towards Selina. 'For some reason he is intrigued by you, Selina.'

'You're ruining everything,' Catherine repeated, her voice low and dangerous, her words now directed at Selina. 'He is my future fiancé and you are jealous. No doubt you are fast realising I am to have a vastly superior life to the one of drudgery that awaits you.'

'We can turn this to our advantage,' Sir William said, ignoring Catherine's outburst.

'How? *I* am supposed to marry Lord Leven. He is reserved with me. I expect she's said something horrible to him about me.'

'What is there between you and Lord Leven?' Her

father's eyes bored into her and Selina struggled to keep her expression neutral.

'Nothing.'

Catherine snorted.

'Quiet,' Sir William snapped. 'We do not have long.' He fixed his gaze on Selina again and she felt the weight of his question.

She thought of when she and Lord Leven had first met, the moment his body had collided with hers and he'd knocked her to the ground. From that very first moment she had felt a spark between them, something indescribable but undeniable.

'There is nothing between us,' Selina said. 'I have spoken to him a few times, that is all. Pleasant conversations.'

'You're trying to steal him from me,' Catherine said.

'Go through to the dining room, Catherine. I need to speak to Selina alone.'

'But…'

'Now.'

With a pout and a swish of her dress Catherine left the room.

'You are unhappy, I think,' Sir William said. He was an astute man, hard in character but shrewd. 'What is it you want, Selina?'

'I want to go home. Coming here was a mistake.'

Her father nodded. Part of her still wanted him to deny it, to take her into his arms and assure her she was a loved and valued member of the family. Even though she had resigned herself to the fact that was never going to happen, it still hurt every time he disappointed her.

'I expect you wish to see your sister. Your true sister.'

'More than anything else.'

'I can arrange that. I can organise a carriage to take you home, give you money to pay for the accommodation you will need on the way.'

She waited, knowing there would be a catch. Her father was not going to offer something like this without there being conditions attached.

'First you must convince Lord Leven to marry Catherine. I want you to use whatever influence you have with him to show him Catherine's attributes, to make sure he is eager to form an alliance with our family. Can you do that?'

She didn't want to deceive Lord Leven. From what she knew of the man he seemed decent, far too kind to be lumbered with Catherine as a wife, but she was aware the negotiations were already halfway there. Lord Leven was already planning on marrying Catherine, so her role would be merely to help things go smoothly. In return she would finally be free. In a few short weeks she could be on her way back to England, back to see her sister, back where she belonged. Then she could start to work out what she was going to do with her life.

'I doubt Lord Leven will ask my opinion on the matter,' Selina said.

'Perhaps not outright, but I do not doubt he is a clever man. By all accounts his father left nothing but debts and chaos. Lord Leven has worked hard these last ten years to make enough money to start rebuilding this once-grand family. He knows the importance of inside information. I expect he plans to use your connection to our family to find out whatever he can. All you need to do is be complimentary about Catherine.'

Selina swallowed hard. It was one thing stopping herself from saying anything terrible about her half-sister, but quite another to be effusively complimentary.

'Can you do that?'

Thinking of going home, Selina nodded.

'Good. We have a deal. You will use your influence with Lord Leven to ensure this alliance between our families is the best it can possibly be and, once he and Catherine are married, I will send you back to England with a small annual allowance.'

He held out his hand for her to shake and, as she

took his cool, dry hand in her own, she felt as though she had just made a deal with the devil.

'I think it is time to eat,' Sir William said.

Selina followed her father out the door, her stomach flipping as she entered the dining room. She did not want to deceive Lord Leven, but he had already made his decision to marry Catherine. Surely it would not be too terrible if she spent a few weeks hiding her true feelings about her half-sister.

'Selina, you take the seat the other side of Lord Leven,' Sir William said, touching his wife on the shoulder. 'You come sit next to me, my dear. Lord Leven is in safe hands with Catherine and Selina.'

Selina felt Lord Leven's eyes on her as she sat, her hands trembling as she smoothed her skirts down under the table.

Dinner had been an ordeal that Selina wished to never repeat. Her cheeks ached from smiling a smile that was as fake as the paste jewels she wore at her neck. It was a relief when the last plate had been cleared and it was only a matter of time before Sir William suggested he and Lord Leven retire to the study for a drink and the start of gentle negotiations. Lady Kingsley and Catherine would move to the drawing room and Selina would finally be able to make her excuses and slip upstairs.

'Let us all go through to the drawing room,' Lady Kingsley said. 'There will be plenty of time for you gentlemen to talk business in the coming days, but this evening let us enjoy one another's company.'

Selina felt her heart sink and it was all she could do to stop herself from groaning out loud.

Lord Leven stood, turning to Catherine and offering her his arm as was expected. Selina fell into step behind them, wondering if she could get away with hiding away in the corner and playing the piano. She had never really enjoyed the piano much when she was a girl, never taken advantage of the opportunities to practise like her sister had, but she was competent and very happy to play now if it meant it got her out of more awkward conversation.

'Miss Shepherd, perhaps you could tell me a little more about the south coast. I have travelled a fair distance in my time, but never to the south of England,' Lord Leven said, looking back at her.

Selina saw Catherine's face cloud over. It was not the first time Lord Leven had tried to include Selina in the conversation and she wished he would stop. Everything would be much easier if they focused on Catherine and how perfect a wife she would make for him.

'It is beautiful. The scenery is dramatic, chalk or sandstone cliffs jutting out into the sea and behind them rolling green hills scattered with sheep.' Selina glanced at Catherine, who was taking the opportunity to glower at her while Lord Leven was engaged in listening to Selina.

'Perhaps you might play for us, Selina,' Lady Kingsley said, guiding everyone else into their positions.

'Gladly, Lady Kingsley.' She hurried over to the piano and quickly leafed through the sheets of music, settling on a slow, soothing piece that she had played many times before. She wanted to bury herself in music, to bend her head and block out the conversation between Lord Leven and Catherine, but her sense of curiosity was too strong.

As she played she listened, realising Catherine had been correct when she had called Selina jealous earlier. She *was* jealous. Catherine was poised to marry a titled and respected man, to live her life as the Countess of Leven. Everything had been organised for her, all she had to do was ensure she did nothing so terrible it changed Lord Leven's mind. It felt unfair—here she was, unsure what was in store for her next. She wished to visit her sister, to spend some time in Sarah's soothing company, but beyond that Selina had no idea what she might do with her life. The thought was depressing and as she tried to rally she missed a note, an E ringing out instead of an F and sounding far too loud.

'Please,' Catherine said, throwing a filthy look at Selina. 'You are giving me a headache with that discordant tripe.'

'I am sorry,' Selina murmured, biting back the retort she wished to say. Sir William would not be impressed if she started arguing with Catherine in front of their guest, especially not after she had promised to do whatever she could to make the match a success.

'I think you play very well, Miss Shepherd,' Lord Leven said and Selina's eyes widened. Although she did not know him well, she could tell he was a kind man, one who did not like to sit by and watch those little injustices in the world. She grimaced, thinking of how poorly suited he would be to Catherine.

Miss Kingsley reddened as she realised she had sounded rude to Lord Leven and she clutched at his arm, her mouth opening but no words coming out. Eventually she managed to speak, 'I think I shall retire,' she said, smiling sweetly. 'I really do have a headache and it is making me crotchety.'

There was a momentary silence and then Lord Leven bowed. 'I do hope you recover swiftly, Miss Kingsley.' Disappointment flashed in Catherine's eyes and Selina could see her half-sister had miscalculated. No doubt she wanted Lord Leven to protest, to press her to stay, perhaps to even suggest a private walk in the gardens or to play a duet on the piano.

'Are you sure you cannot stay?' Lady Kingsley asked sharply.

'Let her rest,' Sir William said. 'There is plenty of time for Catherine and Lord Leven to get to know one another. Perhaps you might escort Catherine on a trip around the local area in the coming days.'

Lord Leven bowed his head in acquiescence. 'Of course. I will call on you soon, Miss Kingsley.'

Catherine hesitated for a moment longer and then turned and left the room.

An awkward little silence followed, broken only when Lord Leven spoke.

'I wonder, it has been a long time since I was inside this house. Would it be too much of an imposition to have a look around? I would be interested to see what changes you have made.'

Sir William spread his hands and gave a magnanimous ushering gesture. 'By all means. We would be very happy for you to look around. Perhaps you could accompany Lord Leven, Selina?'

'Of course,' Selina murmured, surprised by the turn of events as well as the warmth in her father's voice. Ever since she had first thought to seek him out after her mother's death and the revelation that her father was not a faceless army officer, long dead, as her mother had told her, she had dreamed of a loving relationship filled with care and sentimentality.

That dream was what had made her stick around for so long when she knew she should have abandoned the idea of a doting family long ago. She hated that at the first sign of affection she was ready to forget all the past hurts, even when she knew her father was only being reasonable because she was finally useful to him.

'Do you think...?' Lady Kingsley began. She looked worried and would never normally openly question her husband's word.

Sir William waved an indulgent hand. 'We are inside our home and soon Lord Leven will be family. There is no need to worry about propriety, I trust Lord Leven completely.'

'We shall only be a few minutes,' Lord Leven confirmed, offering his arm to Selina.

They walked out of the dining room into the spacious hall. Despite it being where Selina was currently staying and Lord Leven was only a guest, he firmly led the way, taking her this way and that through the maze of downstairs rooms.

'This is a strange thing to do,' Selina said eventually.

Lord Leven shrugged. 'This whole evening has been strange.'

'You noticed?'

'Are they always that odd?'

Selina took her time before replying, reminding herself that she was meant to be enticing Lord Leven to marry into the family, not scaring him away.

'They have their quirks, like all families do.'

'Mine certainly does.'

'You said you don't have much family left locally.'

He shrugged. 'A lot of people have left. It became very difficult to make a living up here and there were better opportunities elsewhere, but there are still a few relatives around.'

'No one close though?'

'My mother lives close by.'

Selina cocked her head. 'You didn't mention her earlier.'

Lord Leven leaned in closer and lowered his voice, his breath tickling her ear. 'Can I tell you a secret? I don't trust Sir William one little bit.'

'Ah. Surely that will make the negotiations to marry Catherine a little difficult.'

'I doubt he trusts me either.' Lord Leven shrugged. 'We will get there in the end, but until we do the less he knows about me the better. I do not want him to have anything to use as leverage.' It explained why all his answers at dinner had been vague.

'You are set on marrying Catherine, then.'

'Yes,' he said without hesitation. 'As long as Sir William delivers on the promises he has made.'

Selina exhaled, allowing herself to let go of some of the guilt she felt for agreeing to her father's proposition of helping make this marriage happen. Lord Leven was already convinced so her being vaguely complimentary about Catherine was not going to make any difference whatsoever.

'This is where you grew up?' Selina said as he paused outside a comfortable sitting room. It was a cosy room, filled with sunshine in the early morning with a good view of the parkland to the left of the house.

'Yes. I spent my childhood here.'

'You have happy memories?'

'Some. Some less happy.'

'This is the house you want to raise your own family in? To reclaim Taigh Blath for the Thomsons?'

He started to speak and then stopped after a moment, eyeing her curiously.

'I do not know where your loyalties lie, Miss Shepherd. You are a very easy person to talk to, but I have to remind myself you are affiliated to the Kingsleys.'

'I would not relay things you had told me in confidence to Sir William,' Selina said, hurt by the accusation. She pressed her lips together, telling herself that despite the feeling she had that she had known Lord Leven a long time, in reality they had only spoken for a few minutes on a couple of occasions. She felt at ease with him, but that did not mean anything, not really. Whatever fantasies she had spun in her head the night before were not real. Lord Leven's loyalties were not to her.

'It is not the house,' he said, his eyes fixed on hers, bright with intensity. 'It is the land.'

'There is something special about the land?'

'For generations my ancestors have lived here, taking care of the land, ensuring we do not take away more than we give back. When my father died and I had to sell Taigh Blath, I lost the land that my friends and family lived on, relied on for their food, where their homes were built.'

'The land is still there, though.'

'But the people are not. Sir William sees the estate as a way of making money.' He held up his hands before she could interrupt. 'It is not a criticism. He has no ties here, it is not his family living in the cottages or fishing in the loch. He thinks like a businessman, working the land for profit.'

'You are not interested in profit?'

'Only to put back into the estate. Of course, there needs to be income, profit made from farming and rents, but I have no interest in hoarding money in a bank. The proceeds from the income can be re-invested in the estate, pay for repairs, ensure there is enough set aside for the harder years—the bad harvests or when the livestock are decimated by some disease.'

'You would keep nothing for yourself.'

He smiled at her then and Selina's heart felt as though it skipped a beat.

'I am no saint, Miss Shepherd. Nor am I a cruel man. I will not make my wife live as a pauper, but I have learned these last ten years that it is possible to live a fulfilling life without the trappings of wealth.'

'I think you are marrying into the wrong family,' Selina said, the words out before she could stop them. A hand flew to her mouth and she had to suppress a groan. Sometimes the words slipped out before she could censor them.

Lord Leven grinned at her. 'Do not fear, Miss Shepherd, I will not repeat your words. I am well aware my future bride and I will likely have very different priorities. I do not wish her to be miserable, stuck out here in the Scottish countryside, but I have to think of everyone else who is relying on me.'

'I am sure Catherine will soon adapt to her new way of life,' Selina said, hoping to salvage something from her mistake. 'She is eager to learn.'

'We can hope,' he murmured, turning away from Selina and to her surprise stepping towards the staircase that led up from the ground floor in the east wing. It was less grand than the main staircase, but still swept up for three floors, allowing access to the entire east wing. It was a peculiarity of the house that you could not access any of the upstairs floors of the east wing from the main section, but had to go down one set of stairs and up another.

Glancing over her shoulder Selina followed Lord Leven up, surprised when he stepped into an airy room which was devoid of much furniture.

'Is this room something special?' she asked, wondering why they had bypassed so many others and come here instead.

'When I was young I always thought I would keep my study here.'

'Not the big room next to the drawing room downstairs?'

'That was my father's study. I wanted something different.'

'Why this room?'

'Come here.' He ushered her over to the window, waiting until she stepped in close to continue. As Selina moved closer she felt the breath catch in her chest. There were still a few inches between them, anyone looking in from outside would not think there was any impropriety, yet Selina was aware of the shift in the atmosphere.

'You can see all the way along the shore of Loch

Leven from here. It's the only room in the house with such an uninterrupted view.'

It was beautiful...mesmerisingly so. Selina leaned forward, resting her arms on the windowsill, her breath steaming the glass. She took her time looking, trying to understand what it was about this place that inspired such devotion from Lord Leven.

Outside the sunlight glinted off the surface of the loch and the trees swayed gently in the breeze. The land was a rich green, the soil fertile and on a distant hill Selina could see a flock of sheep dotted across the grass.

After a minute she straightened and took a step back, her body colliding with the solid form of Lord Leven. Selina exhaled sharply and spun to face him, her hands raising instinctively, her fingers brushing against his chest. The sounds of the household faded and for a moment it felt as though Selina and Lord Leven were the only two people in the world. She knew she should step away, that to linger for even a second more was dangerous, but she was rooted to the spot, her body refusing to obey even the simplest of commands.

She was consumed with thoughts of kissing him and against her better judgement she swayed forward, raising up on to the balls of her feet, her lips now just a few tantalising inches from his. She recognised the same desire she felt mirrored in Lord Leven's eyes and her body thrummed with anticipation as his fingers came up to touch her cheek. Her hands still rested on his chest and even through the layers of material she could feel the strong, steady beat of his heart.

'Miss Shepherd,' he murmured.

Just the sound of her name on his lips sent a shiver through her body. In that moment Selina would have abandoned everything she had ever been taught about the value of a young woman's virtue. She wanted to feel his lips on hers, his body pressed against her naked skin.

Selina closed her eyes and tilted her chin up ever so slightly, her lips parting. She waited for Lord Leven's lips to brush against hers, but they never came. Lord Leven groaned, his fingers dropping from her face, and Selena felt a miniscule fall in temperature as he stepped away. Her eyes shot open and her cheeks flushed. It was an outright rejection and it stung sharply as if she had been slapped.

Lord Leven cleared his throat, taking a moment to compose himself before turning back to her. Selina was fighting back tears and she desperately tried to hide how upset she felt.

'Miss Shepherd, I...'

A glare from Selina silenced him.

'It's getting late,' she said, 'I should return to Sir William and Lady Kingsley.'

Without waiting to hear Lord Leven's response she spun and fled the room, cursing under her breath as in her haste her hip bounced off the door frame.

Chapter Seven

Callum had not been back to Taigh Blath for three days and his visit was long overdue. He had promised to take Miss Kingsley for a walk around the local area and since the dinner party he had received two notes pressing him to confirm when his next visit would be.

This morning he had woken with a renewed sense of determination. The marriage needed to be finalised, the land returned to the Thomson family and all thoughts of Miss Shepherd banished. He had been working towards this moment for ten years. Ten long, hard years as he had clawed his way back from the financial mess his father had left him in. All through those ten years he had never once wavered in his purpose. He could not let one pretty young woman send him off track now.

'You look troubled,' Catriona Thomson, Countess of Leven, said. She stood from where she was sitting at the kitchen table, chopping vegetables ready for dinner.

'I'm off to Taigh Blath,' Callum said, bending down to place a gentle kiss on his mother's hair. Her movements were stiff and slow now, the last decade having taken a toll on her health. She was sixty, with long grey hair that sat in a plait down her back, her skin clear and bright, but with a network of delicate wrinkles.

She sighed and looped and arm around his waist, holding him to her for a moment. 'You do not have to go, Callum.'

'Of course I do. Even I baulk at the idea of marrying a woman I have only spent one evening with.'

'You know I don't mean that. You don't have to go at all. Forget this plan, forget marrying this girl. We are comfortable here, no one will begrudge you putting yourself first for once.'

He did not reply. It was an argument they'd had many times over the last few months and neither of them was going to change their opinion. He had inherited his father's stubbornness, but his mother was no meek and mild lady, and it meant when they clashed neither would back down. Thankfully disagreements were few and far between—after living abroad for so many years he was mindful to appreciate everything he had missed while he was away.

'You should at least bring her to meet your family. She will become part of our community as soon as you marry.'

Callum looked around the comfortable cottage. It was modest in size, but there was no getting past the fact the little residence only contained four rooms. He had a similar dwelling close by. It had everything he needed, but he could not see Miss Kingsley being impressed by the basic cottage.

There was also his desire not to mix these two worlds before he really needed to. One day very soon he would have to finally accept his life was going to change irreversibly, but he was keen to hold off this moment until he had exchanged vows with Miss Kingsley.

'I'll think about it.'

'Stubborn,' Lady Leven said, shaking her head. 'You always were stubborn, like your father.'

'Not just my father.'

'I am well known for my easy-going attitude and adaptability,' she said with a little smile.

'Hmm.' Callum kissed her once more on the head and then called Hamish to his side. The dog had a favourite spot by the fire in Lady Leven's cottage and even on a day like today where there was no need for a fire in the grate he still liked to curl up in the same place.

'Don't take her on a treacherous path. I think sometimes you forget how difficult the terrain can be if you did not grow up scampering over these hills.'

'I will take her on a stroll no more strenuous than a walk in a park.'

He left the cottage, appreciating the cool breeze on his face. It was approaching the best part of the year in Ballachulish, but the weather was always unreliable. Sometimes June could bring hot weather one afternoon followed by a week of storms and a wind that would be at home whipping across the frozen plains of Canada. Today the sky was overcast but the temperature pleasant and he hoped they would have an hour or two of fine weather to go for a stroll before the rain set in later in the afternoon.

He walked briskly, Hamish trotting along by his side happily. As he walked he let his eyes roam over the land he loved so much, taking in the hills and the loch in the distance, revelling in the deep sense of satisfaction he got from being out here in the open.

As he approached Taigh Blath he glanced up and saw a figure at one of the upstairs windows. Even from a distance and with the distortion of the glass he knew it was Miss Shepherd. Involuntarily his muscles tensed and his breathing became a little shallower. He thought back to the moment in the upstairs room of the east wing of the house. He'd come dangerously close to kissing Miss Shepherd there and not for the first time.

The door opened before he could knock and Miss Kingsley herself stepped out to greet him. She was dressed ready for a gentle stroll, with a bonnet on her head and dainty shoes on her feet—hardly the footwear for the local terrain. Silently he recalculated the best route to take so as not to tax Miss Kingsley in her unsuitable footwear.

'Good afternoon,' he greeted her, forcing a smile on to his face. Apart from her abrupt, sometimes rude treatment of Miss Shepherd, Miss Kingsley had not done anything to offend him and he needed to make more of an effort to be pleasant and welcoming to her. Sir William did not seem to be the sort of man to be influenced by others, but if Miss Kingsley petitioned her father to push through the marriage on her behalf then it would hopefully mean the negotiations became a little easier.

'Good afternoon, shall we go?' She spoke quietly, touching his elbow and pressing him to turn away from the house.

'I trust you are well, Miss Kingsley?'

'Very well. Shall we leave?' she said, glancing over the shoulder.

He hesitated. 'Do we not need a chaperon?'

'Catherine,' Lady Kingsley's voice rang out from

the house. Miss Kingsley pressed her lips together in displeasure. 'Miss Shepherd will accompany you. It would be improper to be out alone with Lord Leven, even though soon he will be family.'

Miss Shepherd stepped out and as her boots touched the ground outside the sun appeared from behind a cloud and shone down on her, illuminating her like a creature from heaven.

Callum silently scoffed at his own thoughts and firmly pushed them away. Hamish barked and ran to Miss Shepherd, jumping up to receive a scratch behind his ears that left the dog's tail wagging.

'You spoil him,' Callum murmured.

'Nonsense. A handsome, good boy like him deserves some love and attention,' Miss Shepherd said, not looking up.

'He's a working dog.'

'Even working dogs can enjoy a little petting.'

'Lord Leven asked you to leave the dog alone, Selina. Leave. Him. Alone.' Miss Kingsley spoke sharply, reaching out to tug at the other young woman when she did not straighten immediately.

Miss Shepherd raised an eyebrow, looked directly at Miss Kingsley and ruffled Hamish's ears a final time before stepping away. Hamish barked happily and fell in beside Miss Shepherd as if she had been his companion all his life.

'Have a pleasant walk,' Lady Kingsley said before turning to Miss Shepherd and saying pointedly, 'I expect you will want to give Catherine and Lord Leven some privacy while remaining within a respectable distance.'

Fighting the urge to flee, Callum instead escorted Miss Kingsley down the drive away from Taigh Blath, aware of Miss Shepherd trailing behind somewhere with Hamish trotting happily alongside her. Once or twice he glanced back, but in the whole he managed to focus mainly on the young woman beside him rather than the one he wanted to be walking beside. Miss Shepherd was studiously avoiding eye contact with him and the further they walked the more distance she put between them.

He led Miss Kingsley on a gentle walk through the countryside, making sure he kept to well-trodden paths and gentle inclines only. As they walked he pointed out the local beauty spots, of which there were many.

'I've always loved this view,' Callum said, pausing to point out the way the hills rolled down to the edge of the loch and the trees lined the opposite bank.

Miss Kingsley scrunched up her nose and looked around dubiously. 'Is it always so…muddy?'

Callum laughed and then realised she was not joking. 'We have a fair bit of rain in the Highlands, so there is always a little mud underfoot,' he said, his voice measured. Despite years living in the wilderness of Canada, spending long periods on his own, Callum normally found it easy to talk to people, but he was struggling with Miss Kingsley. He told himself it didn't matter they had nothing in common, with time surely she would come to love the lochs and the glens almost as much as he did.

'It is spring, nearly summer. Please tell me it doesn't rain all summer long.'

'Even in London it must rain in the summer months sometimes.'

'Of course, but there is much to divert oneself with in London. Shopping and going to balls and attending the opera.' She looked at him with sudden interest. 'Do you have any culture up here?'

Callum bristled, fighting to keep the note of irritation from his voice. He knew what she meant—she was asking if there were social events, plays, operas, such as she was used to—but it felt as though she was judging Ballachulish and its people as uncultured.

'I dare say there are such things in Glasgow, perhaps even in Oban, but we are a little rural out here in Ballachulish for it to be worthwhile to build an opera house or a theatre. Most people choose to enjoy the natural beauty of the land that surrounds them. They swim in the lochs and take picnics on long walks.'

Miss Kingsley looked horrified for a moment before fixing her face into a more suitable expression.

'Come on, let us get closer to the loch.'

It was a bad move, for as they approached the water's edge they were attacked by swarms of midges. They flitted around their faces, landing on their bare skin and tangling in their hair.

'We should climb higher,' Callum called out, knowing the midges preferred it close to the water. Up on the hillside they would likely escape the swarms.

'Yes, please let us go higher,' Miss Shepherd said, quickly pressing her lips together against the swarms of tiny flies. It was the first time she had spoken since they'd left Taigh Blath and she'd only now broken her silence out of necessity.

Miss Kingsley nodded in agreement, not wanting to open her mouth and invite in the horrible little creatures. She looked miserable, with lifeless strands of hair stuck to her forehead under her bonnet and the first red bumps from the midge bites visible on her cheeks. Callum's heart sank. His plan had been to show Miss Kingsley the best of his country, to make her fall in love with the nature and the wildlife and the people, starting with one of his favourite views in all the world. Instead he was afraid he'd traumatised the young woman.

She had made her views clear on the lack of cultural and social events in Ballachulish and Callum had the sinking feeling that she would try to persuade him to set up their primary residence elsewhere once they were married. Perhaps in Edinburgh or, even worse, London.

Quickly they climbed, Hamish darting backwards and forward, having a great time as the walk turned from gentle stroll into more strenuous hike. After five minutes they had escaped the swarms of midges and after ten he called a stop to the march.

Miss Kingsley flopped down and pulled her bonnet from her head, closing her eyes for a moment. She looked exhausted and close to tears. Callum laid a gentle hand on her shoulder and after a moment she opened her eyes and looked up at him.

'I'm sorry. The midges are unpredictable. I wanted to show you the view, not torture you.'

'What disgusting things they are. I do not know how you can bear to live here being bombarded by horrible little flies all the time.' Her voice was sharp, her tone accusatory, but Callum could see she was genuinely upset about how the morning had turned out.

'You do get used to it,' Callum said softly. 'The hills, the mud, the midges. I am sure it seems very different right now to the world you are used to, but with time...'

Miss Kingsley looked up at him and raised an eyebrow. 'I do not plan to let the failings of the Scottish countryside affect our planned union, my lord, but I do not think I can pretend that I will ever get used to any of this.' She waved a hand vaguely around her, crossing her arms in front of her chest and pressing her lips together firmly.

Callum breathed out slowly before speaking again. Everything seemed difficult with Miss Kingsley. Every time they spoke their conversation was stilted and he realised they had absolutely nothing in common. He had to tell himself that it didn't matter, people all over the world married when they barely knew one another, he had never fantasised about falling in love, so he would just have to put up with Miss Kingsley's moans and hope that once she had settled in she would see the positives of her new life in Scotland.

'We can rest here for a while before taking another route down. That way we will avoid the worst of the midges at the water's edge.'

He glanced up, his eyes searching for Miss Shepherd who had not come to join them. She was standing a little distance away, hands on hips, surveying the view.

'Excuse me one moment,' he said to Miss Kingsley, moving away before she could protest. Over the years he had learned to move quietly. In his youth his father had loved hunting and often would take Callum with him as a sharp pair of eyes to spot the elusive stags he liked to shoot and display on the walls of Taigh Blath. As Callum grew older he found an excuse to eschew the hunting trips, but the skill of moving silently through any environment was one that had served him well over the years. 'It is beautiful, is it not?' he said quietly as he stopped a pace behind Miss Shepherd.

She did not move, did not turn to face him. Instead he was left to stare at the back of her neck. Despite Miss Kingsley sitting only a few feet away he had the urge to reach out and touch the soft skin, to twist the loose hairs around his fingers and feel their silky smoothness. He reprimanded himself immediately and as penance looked back over his shoulder and gave Miss Kingsley a half-smile.

'It is beautiful,' she conceded after half a minute of silence.

Finally she turned to face him and he was surprised to see there were tears in her eyes. He reached out, this time unable to stop himself, and took her hand, thankful his actions were shielded from Miss Kingsley's view by his broad back.

'Is it the midges?'

She laughed and shook her head.

'Is it me?'

After that question her eyes snapped up to meet his and he saw the mixture of hurt and longing in them. He hadn't wanted to step away from her in the east wing of Taigh Blath—every single fibre of his body had wanted to take her in his arms and kiss her. He could not explain this attraction he felt. Miss Shepherd was pretty, that much was undeniable, but he had met countless pretty young women over the years that he had never given a second thought to. Yet here was Miss Shepherd, appearing at the most important moment of his life so far, who he could not stop thinking about.

'No.' She turned away abruptly, looking out longingly at the view. After a minute she glanced back and, when she saw he had not moved, she sighed. 'In many ways this is a very different view from back home, but there is something about it that reminds me of the places I loved in Sussex.'

'You are pining for familiar shores.'

'I am.' She gave a little, humourless laugh. 'Although if I went back in time and told the me from a year ago I wanted nothing more than to breath in the salty sea air as I climbed the winding streets to the Firehills in Hastings, the me back then would have laughed.'

'I think it is natural to want to experience a little of what the rest of the world has to offer us,' Callum said, remembering his excitement when he had first stepped off the ship on to Canadian shores. His plan had always been to return home, but those first few months had been an adventure he'd been glad to live through.

'I was dismissive of our home, our life in Hastings. I think my sister would have stayed there after our mother's death if I had asked her to. Now...' She trailed off.

'Now it feels as though you do not have a home?'

She nodded, the tears glinting in her eyes again, although she was able to stop them from spilling on to her cheeks.

'Will the Kingsleys offer you a place, once they return to London?'

Miss Shepherd looked at him in horror, so aghast at his suggestion that she took a stumbling step back. 'I am leaving soon, much sooner than the Kingsleys.'

He felt a sense of disappointment at her declaration, even though he had no right to feel anything about her travel intentions.

'Where will you go?'

She shrugged.

'Your father is deceased?'

There was a moment's pause before she nodded, her eyes sliding away from his.

'My sister will take me in, I will not be left on the streets.'

'Do I sense a reluctance there? Do you not get on with your sister?'

'No. Sarah is the best person I have ever met. She is kind and patient and wonderful,' Miss Shepherd paused for a moment to formulate her next sentence. 'She has married well and she would like nothing more than to give me security and a home for life.'

'That is not what you want?'

Miss Shepherd turned to face him fully, her eyes searching his face. He felt naked beneath her gaze, as if she were assessing the depths of his soul. 'I want something of my own. I do not know as yet what that is, but I know it will not be a life where I am reliant on my sister's charity. I want more. Do you understand?'

'Yes.' It was all the reply needed. He had always been driven by an indescribable urge to strive for more, to stretch for something that was just out of reach. Over the years this drive had served him well, going from destitute heir, scrabbling to find a way to satisfy all his father's debtors, to a man who was about to restore to his family the majority of their lands and estates. 'You will find it, whatever it is you are looking for.'

'It would be simpler if I knew what that was.'

'It would,' he said, leaning in closer and catching a hint of her scent, a subtle floral perfume. 'But perhaps less fun.'

Her eyes flicked to his lips and then back up to look directly into his. As he watched her he saw her cheeks flush and her pupils widen and it was all he could do to stop himself from stepping up and kissing her. It was intoxicating, knowing a woman, especially a woman he himself felt an intense attraction to, desired him so much.

For the first time he wondered what his life would be like if he gave in to his desires and kissed her right there on the hill overlooking the loch. The marriage to Miss Kingsley would be called off, which in itself would not be a great loss. Instead he would get to wake up to Miss Shepherd beside him every day, to tumble her into his bed every evening.

With great difficulty he looked away. It was cruel to do anything else. His desire for her could not overshadow what he had been working towards for so long. With a stab of guilt he realised he had been longing for one woman while his intended sat only a few feet away.

'What are you talking about?' Miss Kingsley said from her position on the ground a little distance away.

'The view,' Miss Shepherd said, her voice light and breezy. Callum had to study her carefully to see the evidence that she was as shaken by their encounter as he was.

'We should start making our descent,' Callum said, examining the clouds. He wasn't overly concerned about the weather, but the clouds were gathering slowly on the horizon. An impending storm was a good excuse to get Miss Shepherd and Miss Kingsley back to Taigh Blath as quickly as possible. He might even insist he and Sir William sat down and concluded their negotiations. Once the wedding date was set perhaps he would stop trying to self-sabotage with the delectable Miss Shepherd and would be able to focus on his bride-to-be.

'Perhaps I could hold your arm, Lord Leven, the ground is a little uneven underfoot.'

'It would be easier if you had worn something akin to sensible shoes,' Miss Shepherd said under her breath.

'We don't all have clod-hopping great feet like you,' Miss Kingsley retorted sharply. 'You cannot expect a gently bred young woman to own a pair of ugly boots as you do, Selina.'

Callum wondered at the animosity between the two young women. They were of a similar age and, if Miss Shepherd was a distant relative of the Kingsleys, they had some sort of family connection. Their dislike of one another ran deep, that much was obvious, it was more than the bickering you sometimes saw between friends and relatives.

'Let us get down to level ground before any rain comes, otherwise those pretty shoes of yours will be ruined,' Callum said.

They walked in silence for a few minutes until Miss Shepherd called out from behind, 'Is this truly your favourite view in the world, Lord Leven?'

'It is, Miss Shepherd—do you think you could beat it?'

Coming level with him and Miss Kingsley, she took a moment to shade the light from her eyes.

'It is magnificent,' she conceded. 'And you have an advantage over me. You have travelled.'

'A little. Much of the world is still a mystery to me.'

'I have been to many of the counties in southern England,' Miss Kingsley said, straining her neck forward to try to block out Miss Shepherd from the conversation.

'Many more than I have, then,' Callum said. 'The furthest south I have been is Manchester.'

'You've never set foot in London?'

'No. Never. My father talked about taking me when I was younger, but it never happened.'

'Surely as an adult…?' Miss Kingsley asked, her expression stunned.

'I spent most of my adult life away from home, in

the wilds of Canada. When I returned I was in no rush to leave the people and the places I had missed so much.'

She beamed, her eyes alight with joy, seeming much happier than she had on the rest of the walk. 'You will *love* London. Many people do not want to leave; even once the Season is over and some people go back to their country estates, it is still the most wonderful city.'

Callum debated whether he needed to say something to Miss Kingsley about where they would live. As much as he wanted this marriage to go ahead, to finally restore some of his family's lands, he also had to acknowledge he was taking responsibility for Miss Kingsley along the way. She would be his wife, his to look after and keep happy. Starting with a deception would not be ideal.

'You do understand once we are married we will live here, in Ballachulish.' His voice was gentle, but even so Miss Kingsley looked as though he had stabbed her in the gut.

'Well, yes, but...'

He shook his head. 'We will live here. Of course, you would be free to travel south to visit your parents, your friends, but we would reside here in the Highlands.'

'Surely you might consider Edinburgh...?'

'No. *This* is home, Miss Kingsley and as Earl of Leven I have a responsibility to my people here. I cannot abandon them.'

'You went to Canada for years.'

'With the aim of returning with enough funds to start to buy back the land my family lost.'

Miss Kingsley pouted, her brows drawn into a frown.

'I truly think if you give it a chance you will learn to like it here.'

She let out a little frustrated sigh. 'Very well,' she said, her voice hard. 'I understand. Please do not think this will dampen my enthusiasm for our union, my lord.' It was the first time she had spoken so openly about their impending engagement and Callum saw there was a determination in her eyes that he had not been aware of before.

Miss Kingsley looked as though she were going to say more, but suddenly gave a little cry of pain, her hand tugging on Callum's sleeve. He tensed his arm, reaching to support her with his other hand, but it was too late to save her from the twist of her ankle. The delicate, unsuitable shoe had slipped a little on the path, caught in a small groove and led to her ankle turning in a way it should not.

'Sit down,' he said, leading her over to a small rock. Carefully he pressed at her ankle, grimacing as she winced. This was no ploy of a cunning debutante to excuse a little close contact, no wily way to seduce him. Already he could feel her ankle swelling—soon the pressure from the extra fluid would make it even more difficult for her to walk and the pain would only get worse.

'Is she badly injured?' Miss Shepherd said, dropping to her knees beside him.

'As though you care,' Miss Kingsley said, tears flowing on to her cheeks.

'I wouldn't ever wish you harm, Catherine.'

Miss Kingsley did not reply and after a moment Callum stood. It was too far back to Taigh Blàth for him to carry Miss Kingsley all the way, but he could hardly leave the two young women on the exposed hillside while he went to get some help.

'Can you walk?' Miss Shepherd asked.

He offered Miss Kingsley his arm and pulled her up to her feet, but she cried out as soon as she had to put any weight through the left ankle and after a moment he let her sink back down to the rock.

'Let me carry you down the hill,' he said, cursing himself for allowing her up here in such dainty footwear.

'I do not wish to be a burden,' Miss Kingsley said.

'Not at all.' He slipped his jacket off and rolled up his shirtsleeves. There was no point in remaining fully dressed when there was no one else around to see. 'Would you mind, Miss Shepherd?' He handed the jacket to Miss Shepherd who accepted it, concern etched on her face.

'Will you be able to carry her all the way?' Miss Shepherd said, peering down the path in front of them.

'Why do you always have to be so rude, Selina?' Miss Kingsley snapped. 'I am hardly a giant of a woman.'

'I wasn't commenting on your size.'

'You were insulting Lord Leven's strength, then?'

Miss Shepherd breathed deeply and for a minute it seemed as though she was going to be able to take command of herself and leave Miss Kingsley's jibes without response. Or perhaps not.

'Miss Shepherd,' he said quickly as he saw her open her mouth again. 'Perhaps you could walk on ahead and see if there is anyone passing on the road below. If you continue straight you will come upon it with no issue.'

It was unlikely there would be anyone on the small road, but he did not want to deal with an argument between the two young women while he needed all his strength carrying Miss Kingsley down the hill. Trying not to think about the distance between them and Taigh Blath, instead he focused on lifting Miss

Kingsley into his arms and then putting one foot in front of the other.

Carrying her in this fashion was strangely intimate and he found himself wishing he was walking with Miss Shepherd in his arms.

It was a relief five minutes later when he heard the distant but definite sound of hooves on the road ahead and after another few seconds a rider came into view. Suppressing a groan of relief, he carefully set Miss Kingsley down before straightening and stretching out his back.

As he got closer, the figure became recognisable as Thomas Bruce, a man he had known since childhood. They were a few years apart in age, but he knew Bruce well both from before he had left for Canada and since he had returned and counted him among his closest friends. Callum frowned as he realised Miss Shepherd was seated behind him on the horse, her slender arms wrapped around Bruce's waist, holding on just above the waistband of his kilt. Despite being the one to send her to find help, he felt a spike of jealousy. Ignoring it, he turned back to Miss Kingsley.

'It looks as though Miss Shepherd was successful in her mission.'

'I hear there is a damsel in distress in need of my help,' Bruce called, his accent thick and pure

Highlands. 'I am here, eager and ready to assist.' He vaulted down from the horse and turned to help Miss Shepherd down. Callum dug his fingernails into his hand to stop himself for surging forward and barging the other man out of the way.

'This is Miss Kingsley...' Callum began by way of introduction.

'Ah, yes, the English lass you're due to marry. Pleasure to meet you.'

'Miss Kingsley, this is Mr Bruce.'

Miss Kingsley looked a little taken aback by the gruff effusiveness coming from the big bear of a man and merely smiled weakly.

'I hear you've hurt your ankle and need to get back to Taigh Blath.'

'Taigh Blath?'

'Loch View Lodge,' Callum said smoothly, ignoring Bruce's frown. None of the locals acknowledged the change in name of the old estate and they found it difficult to accept Sir William as the man who owned the land they lived on. Highland hospitality was second to none, but only in the right circumstance.

'Your wish is my command, my little lady,' Bruce said, eyeing up Miss Kingsley and then leading his horse closer. 'Can you climb up or shall I throw you over Bessie's back?'

Miss Kingsley blanched and Callum quickly

stepped forward. 'Allow me,' he said, assisting the young woman closer to the horse.

Bruce mounted quickly and then reached back to pull Miss Kingsley up behind him while Callum boosted her up from below. She looked uncomfortable sitting behind the large man, although not for lack of room. Bessie was a huge horse with a broad back and capable of carrying two at least for short distances.

'You'll have to hold on tight,' Bruce said, looking back over his shoulder. 'I don't bite, not unless you want me to.'

'If there was a single moment in your life to behave and act like a gentleman, this is it,' Callum said, his heart sinking at Miss Kingsley's aghast expression at the situation she found herself in. He leaned in closer to the young woman. 'Bruce is a good man. He would defend your honour until his very last breath. You are in safe hands. He will take you back to the house so your ankle can be seen to as quickly as possible. Miss Shepherd and I will follow behind.'

'Can you not take me?'

'No one else can ride a beast like Bessie. You're safe with me,' Bruce said, patting Miss Kingsley on the leg. The young woman looked as though she were going to jump from the horse, twisted ankle be damned.

Before Miss Kingsley could protest any more Bruce spurred Bessie on and set off at a gentle trot, leaving Callum alone with Miss Shepherd.

'Good work on finding Bruce.'

'I hardly did anything. I stepped on to the road and he nearly ran me down on that great horse of his. He makes quite an impression.'

'Miss Kingsley dinnae seem too happy to be sent off with him.'

'No, I don't expect she was. No doubt she had images of you carrying her home, gazing into her eyes and falling irrevocably in love with her.'

'Ah. Instead I threw her on to the back of a horse with a questionable stranger and sent them off into the wilds of the Highlands together.'

'Hardly the romantic gesture she has been dreaming of.'

'I'm not very good at that stuff,' Callum admitted. For years he had lived a rough life, spending weeks at a time alone with only Hamish for company. Even when he did mix with others it had hardly been polite society, with his companions from all different backgrounds, thrown together in the wilderness of Canada. Many of those men had been running from something, or desperately trying to get back to something they had lost. It felt a world apart from sipping tea in a drawing room with the likes of Miss Kingsley.

'You would have to do a lot more than abandon her to the rough manners of Mr Bruce to deter Catherine from this marriage.'

'She has confided in you?'

'Good lord, no,' Miss Shepherd said with a laugh. 'She would not confide in me if I was the only other person left in the world.' She paused and thought for a moment. 'I think she is very eager to marry you, though. She has been raised to make a good match, to marry well, and in you she sees she can realise that ambition and please her father.'

'So it is not me she wants, specifically.'

'I am sure she was not disappointed when she saw you for the first time,' Miss Shepherd said, a sparkle in her eyes. He liked her like this. She seemed carefree away from the oppressive reach of the Kingsley family. 'But even if you were a decrepit old man with no teeth and only half a head of hair I think she would still be keen to marry you.'

'I am not sure if I should be flattered or insulted.'

'It is a good thing, I think. You and Sir William can go about your negotiations without worrying Miss Kingsley will object to any of the terms.'

'How do I win against Sir William, Miss Shepherd?'

'You wish me to betray family secrets?'

'Merely share a few observations as to Sir William's character.'

She thought for a moment and then turned to him again, her arm brushing against his. The touch was momentary, fleeting, but Callum couldn't concentrate for a full thirty seconds, missing what she said first.

'You are determined to marry Miss Kingsley?'

'I am.'

'Then I do not think there is any harm in telling you a little about Sir William. The quicker your negotiations are completed, the sooner I get to go home.'

He raised an eyebrow in question.

'Sir William promised me he would fund my return trip to England if I helped secure your good opinion of Miss Kingsley.'

'By bickering with her at every opportunity?'

'I never said I was any good at it.'

'You are that keen to leave Scotland?'

'I am that keen to start thinking about the future. For the past year I have been chasing dreams, fixated on something that I now realise was never going to happen.' She glanced up at him, biting her lip. 'I felt guilty about doing it, about deceiving you.'

'No need for any guilt. If anything you have made me question my desire to marry Miss Kingsley, not persuaded me to marry her...' he grinned at her expression of exasperation and leaned in closer '...but I will not tell Sir William that.'

'Then in return I will furnish you with everything you need to know to complete your negotiations.'

It felt odd asking Miss Shepherd, the woman he could not stop thinking about in the most inappropriate ways, to help him secure the knowledge he needed to finalise the details of his marriage to another, but this whole situation was odd.

'Sir William is ruthless and relentless. He is a difficult man to win against. He will promise something and then withdraw it, dangle temptation in your path, make you think you want one thing when you came into the situation thinking you wanted something else entirely.'

'A master manipulator.'

'Exactly. He wins by not ever backing down. He will spend a long time gathering all the information he can so that he knows what is important to the person he is up against and what is less so and then he uses the information to get his own way.'

'You have seen him do this.'

'Countless times in countless situations. He uses the same tactics for both the mundane and the more important.'

Callum thought of his own situation. Sir William

was aware of how important the land and estate was to Callum, so already he was on a back foot.

'You need to meet him head on with information of your own.'

'What sort of information?'

Miss Shepherd hesitated and then must have decided to throw caution to the wind. 'He knows you are eager to gain land and the house in the negotiation for Miss Kingsley's dowry. He will be relatively sure you will concede some of that land if it means you get the house and a portion of the estate. In his mind his job is to ensure he does not give away too much.'

'Already he has spoken about renegotiating what was promised in his letters.'

'You have to counter with your own knowledge of what is important to him.'

'His status,' Callum said.

'Yes. As I understand it, for years he has been trying to gain access to the higher echelons of Society. He has more money than half the dukes and Earls in England. He's even organised a small personal loan for the Prince Regent in years gone by. Yet despite this he is not accepted in their circles. He is hampered by the facts of his birth.'

'I have the family name, the lineage.'

'That is what he wants more than anything else. By marrying Catherine to you, his grandson will be the future Earl of Leven. He cannot change his own pedigree, but this is the next best thing.'

'I can hardly threaten to take away the lure of the title. If I marry Miss Kingsley, then she will become Lady Leven, Countess of Leven.'

Miss Shepherd shrugged. 'Then you had better be good at bluffing. Perhaps convincing Sir William you are ready to walk away. Dangle the promise of a title in front of him and then pull it away.'

'You are a ruthless lass, Miss Shepherd.'

She laughed. 'Before the last year I would have professed to have known nothing about these sorts of negotiations. My time with the Kingsleys has not been full of kindness and cheer, but I now can appreciate the nuances of a good business discussion.'

'An education indeed.'

They were on the flat ground now, walking at a decent pace back towards Taigh Blath. Callum surreptitiously slowed a little, not wanting to be back at the house just yet. He reasoned he wasn't sabotaging the match with Miss Kingsley, merely taking a little innocent pleasure while he could.

As they walked a few fat droplets of rain fell from the sky, splattering the earth in front of them. The clouds had gathered to form a dark blanket and there was no sign of the sun.

Miss Shepherd followed his gaze before searching

the distance for any familiar landmarks that might tell her they were close enough to the house to make a dash for it.

'I think we are going to get wet, Miss Shepherd.'

'Since arriving in Scotland I have ruined two dresses already. If I ruin a third, I will be forced to parade round in my undergarments all day.'

Callum took a moment to savour the mental image of Miss Shepherd walking through the countryside in just a thin cotton slip. In his mind he could see the outline of her curves underneath the delicate white fabric, the swell of her breasts and the pinkish hint of colour at her nipples.

He swallowed hard, forcing himself back to the present. Thoughts such as this were not helpful in the slightest.

'Do we push on and hope the rain is not too heavy?'

Forcing his eyes from hers to take in the sky, he calculated the distance between their current position and Taigh Blath.

'We will be soaked to the skin,' he said as the raindrops began falling in earnest. If they hurried, they could be back at the house in fifteen minutes. Walking for fifteen minutes in the rain would not bother him, although he would rather he had the protection of one of his summer coats instead of the more formal jacket he had worn today, but Miss Shepherd might catch a chill in the rain and he would hate to be responsible for that.

Making a decision, he gripped hold of Miss Shepherd's hand, pulling her gently off the road and on to an overgrown grass path.

'I know where we can shelter, let the worst of the rain go over. If we're lucky, it will only be a short shower.'

They ran now, trying to beat the rain as it began coming down faster and faster, the big drops splattering in the mud underfoot and making the conditions slippery. Callum told himself that was why he was holding Miss Shepherd's hand so tight, even though some part of him knew that was a lie. As he held her hand he imagined what might happen if he kept running, if they left their troubles and responsibilities behind them and just ran until there was nothing but their wants and desires left.

Chapter Eight

Selina was breathing hard by the time they reached the tumble-down little cottage that sat close to the low wall that ran around the perimeter of Sir William's estate. It looked as though it had been abandoned at least ten years earlier and was in a bad state of disrepair. The little garden was overgrown with weeds so tall they reached Selina's waist and part of the roof had slipped, leaving some of the inside open to the elements. Even the front door was hanging on its hinges, the wood rotten and soft around the edges.

'Does this place belong to anyone?' Selina asked, hesitating on the threshold. It was clearly uninhabited, but someone might still own the cottage.

'Mrs Douglas used to live here when I was a boy. She died a year or so before I left for Canada, so the place hasn't been occupied for over a decade.'

'There were no children to take it over?'

'No. Everyone thought she was a spinster. When

we were children my friends and I believed she was a witch, but she was just a lonely old woman who hadn't had the easiest time in life. My mother used to go and visit her towards the end, take her a basket of food and ensure she was comfortable.'

He stepped inside, glad to be out of the worst of the weather, even just for a few minutes. 'When she died a husband appeared. Apparently they had married young and bickered relentlessly. He had walked out sixty years earlier and never returned to the village. The cottage passed to him, of course—even after all that time leading separate lives he was still legally her husband—but after her funeral he left again and didn't return.'

'That's a sad story.'

Miss Shepherd stepped inside, removing the bonnet she had donned a couple of hours earlier to protect her from the sun. Now it was sodden and drooping, a sad testament to the ever-changing weather. She shivered and he saw that despite their rapid dash through the rain her dress was soaked, the material sticking to her skin. The material was a pale blue, nothing fancy, but where it was wet it had gone thin, almost translucent.

Callum swallowed, finding it hard to keep his distance. He wanted to cross the room and run his hands over her body, to scrunch up the wet material and lift it over her head. It was a desire he'd felt before when they'd been alone together, but never so strong as now.

Suddenly the room felt very small and he grappled with his cravat, feeling as though it were tightening around his neck. Miss Shepherd seemed oblivious to his distress, exploring the room with a natural curiosity.

'It feels a little voyeuristic,' she said, peering up the dilapidated stairs. 'Like looking into a life I should know nothing about.'

'Mrs Douglas's husband did not want any of her possessions. Some has been taken over the years, I am sure, but her reputation meant most people were keen to stay away. Ask any of the locals outright and they will tell you they don't believe witches walk among us any more, but most will make the sign of the cross and look away from the cottage if they find themselves nearby.'

'You have been here before, though?'

'I came with my mother a few times while Mrs Douglas was still alive. That dispelled any lingering suspicions that she was anything more than a lonely and destitute old lady.'

'You never found a cauldron, or a black cat?'

She craned her neck up and then curiosity got the better of her as she set her foot on the first step.

Callum lunged forward immediately. The stairs were wooden and had been exposed to the elements for the past decade. The wood was soft and rotten, even where it looked intact, and easily splintered underfoot. Miss Shepherd was petite, but if she put her whole weight on the first step he had no doubt it would crack and splinter. Although she wouldn't fall from a height he had seen the damage rotten wood could do to the flesh.

Quickly he grabbed her, pulling her from the step before it could crack completely. In his haste he spun her round, pressing her up against the outer wall of the cottage.

'I'm sorry,' he said, looking down at her, taking in the eyes wide with surprise. 'The stairs are rotten. I did not want you to hurt yourself.'

'You saved me again, my lord.'

'Callum,' he said. 'Please call me Callum.'

'Callum.' She tested out his name, the hint of a smile pulling at the corners of her lips. He couldn't take his eyes off her, couldn't step away. He took in the delicate curve of her cheek, the long lashes that framed her eyes and the very slight upturn of the end of her nose. This close he could even see the smattering of freckles on her cheeks. He wanted to move in even closer, to count those tiny freckles as he kissed each and every single one.

'I promise I am not normally this accident-prone.'

'Perhaps I make you lose your concentration.'

She stiffened at his comment, looking up into his eyes from under her dark lashes.

'Perhaps you do,' she said.

He could see the rise and fall of her chest quicken slightly and saw the way her lips parted as they had a few days earlier when they had been alone in Taigh Blath. Then he had stepped away, he had mastered his desire, overcome the searing attraction he felt, but today he was not sure if he would be able to be so strong again. Every single fibre in his body was screaming out for him to kiss her.

He shifted ever so slightly, his body moving independently of his mind, pressing in closer, and he heard Miss Shepherd's sharp intake of breath. In that moment he wanted to forget about all his responsibilities, to forget about anything other than the perfect lips of the young woman standing in front of him.

Unable to resist any longer, he moved even closer and kissed her, losing himself in the soft sweetness of her lips.

As she reached up and ran her fingers through his hair he found himself wishing he could stay in this moment for ever. Her body was receptive to his touch, her hips pressing against his and her arms pulling him closer.

'I have wanted to kiss you ever since I first tackled you to the ground at the edge of the loch,' he murmured, pulling away for just a moment. She looked beautiful with her cheeks flushed and her hair in dishevelled ringlets loose around her face. He kissed her again and then revelled in the way she moaned as he trailed his lips down her neck from earlobe to collarbone.

Callum could think of nothing else but the woman in front of him. He did not wish to consider the consequences of what he was doing—for once he was allowing himself to think about only pleasure. His hand caught Miss Shepherd around the waist and he held her tight, wondering if he could rip the wet material of her dress where it clung to her body. He had this almost uncontrollable urge to strip the clothes from her, to reveal what was underneath and then spend the rest of time exploring every inch of her with his fingers and his mouth.

He knew she was an innocent and he knew what he was doing was wrong, but for a few minutes he could not listen to the good and moral part of himself, for a few minutes he was swept away in his own desire.

Miss Shepherd pulled him closer to her, her hand brushing lightly against his groin and causing him to groan loudly. She looked surprised and he realised it had not been a calculated move and the look of shocked innocence made him want her even more.

He kissed her again, his tongue tasting the sweetness of her lips as he pressed her against the wall of the cottage. His fingers searched for the fastenings of her dress and as he found the ties at her back he gripped them forcefully and began to pull. Callum felt as though he were in a dream and for a while he could fool himself that the decisions he was making would not affect anything in real life. All he wanted was to slake the desire that had been building for the past week every time he had set eyes on Miss Shepherd.

As he pulled apart Miss Shepherd's dress at the back he felt the material of her chemise underneath and his fingers were just bunching the damp cotton when Hamish barked, getting up from his position by the door to stand at the threshold.

Callum recoiled as if he had been shot. He looked down at Miss Shepherd, his body filled with shock and immediate regret. He had half-ravished the poor young woman and, even though she had kissed him willingly, was under no illusion that he was the one in the wrong.

'I'm sorry,' he said, running a hand through his hair, unable to stop the expression of horror from spreading across his face. 'I should never have allowed that to happen.'

Miss Shepherd did not move. She looked beautiful even in her dishevelled state, Her hair was falling loose around her shoulders, her dress hanging low, exposing more skin than was acceptable in polite society. Her cheeks were flushed and her lips a deep, rosy red.

She looked up at him and he felt the weight of her distress.

'Miss Shepherd...' he said, wanting more than anything to reach out and take her in his arms again, but knowing if he touched her he would be lost. 'Please, forgive me. I lost control. You have my sincerest apologies.'

She started forward and for a moment he thought she was going to flee the cottage. Thoughts of everything he had risked flooded through him as he was almost overcome with shame. For ten years he had promised everyone who would listen that he would right his father's mistakes, that he would be single minded in his pursuit of restoring the Thomson family fortunes. Those ten years of promises had been forgotten in a single moment with Miss Shepherd. He moved to block her way, all he wanted to do was reason with her, to ask her to forgive his foolishness.

'You are worried I am going to tell someone,' she said, her voice flat.

He stayed quiet, aware he deserved her wrath.

'You are thinking of your marriage to Catherine.' She stepped closer, poking a long finger into his chest, her eyes alive with fury. 'You kiss me, you nearly take my virtue and all you can think about is saving this horrible union you want to make with the Kingsleys.'

'Miss Shepherd...'

She spun away, pushing past him. This time he let her go. As she crossed the threshold, stepping out into the rain, she looked back.

'Have your precious marriage to Catherine. I will not say anything. The quicker you marry, the quicker I can leave this godforsaken place and never come back.'

Before he could stop her she turned and ran, darting out into the heavy rain as if she barely noticed the awful weather.

Callum did not move for a whole minute, his body rigid. It was only when Hamish came and nuzzled against his hand that he was spurred into action.

Cursing under his breath, he hurried out the door of the cottage, shielding his eyes from the rain to try to see Miss Shepherd. A mist had descended as often did later in the afternoon on the unsettled days and the visibility was poor now. He took a moment to look in all directions, wondering if Miss Shepherd knew the way back to the house or if she had just taken off at a run in a bid to get away from him.

Hoping she had at least some sense of the direction of the house, he started to make his way back towards Taigh Blath, his heart heavy. For years he had prided himself on being different to his father. He never drank to excess, limiting himself to at most one glass of liquor of an evening if he was in company. He did not gamble either—his whole life had been shaped by his father's poor business decisions and even poorer skill at the gaming tables.

Ever since he had inherited the title and the responsibility for his people he had vowed he would dedicate his life to restoring the land to them, to bringing the wider family home, for making the area somewhere people wanted to live, somewhere there was plenty of work. Through all the hardships he had suffered in Canada, months of surviving only on what he could catch in the frozen wilderness, weeks without seeing another human, he had stayed strong and focused on the reasons why he was doing it all. Yet one glance at Miss Shepherd and he had risked everything he had worked to put into place.

As the towering height of Taigh Blath came into view he forced himself to push aside the image of hurt and betrayal on Miss Shepherd's face as she saw his regret at their intimacy. There was no excuse for what he had done, it was unforgivable, yet he believed what she had said when she had promised not to tell. It should feel like a victory, like something positive to salvage out of this awful mess he had made, but the heartbreak in her eyes had been so awful he knew he would never forget that moment, or forgive himself for it.

Chapter Nine

With the tears stinging her eyes and clouding her vision, Selina stumbled more than once as she ran from the cottage back towards Taigh Blath. The pain she felt was deep and visceral, as if Lord Leven had reached into her chest and ripped her heart from her body.

'You stupid girl,' she muttered to herself. Once again she had been swept away in the fantasy, despite telling herself she would not become embroiled with Lord Leven. When he had looked at her with that animalistic yearning in his eyes she had felt something throb and pulse deep inside her. She was not naive, she had known they could have no future, yet as he had pulled her from the creaking staircase and pressed her against the wall she had been powerless to resist him.

The kiss had been inevitable, the culmination of all of those fleeting touches and the building attraction they had felt for one another, but it did not excuse it. Lord Leven was determined to marry Catherine, they were practically engaged. Selina should have known no mere physical attraction could make him waver from his path, yet when he had been kissing her she had felt as though it was everything she had ever wanted. Suddenly she had felt a clarity unlike anything she had ever known before. It was intoxicating, the dream that they might get to spend their life in one another's arms, and for a few minutes it had been all Selina had wanted.

Until she'd seen the look of abject horror on Lord Leven's face.

Selina felt the rush of shame and sorrow. Back home she had attended the local dances and had never struggled to fill her dance card. She knew she was attractive enough and hadn't ever thought anyone would look at her with such a look as Lord Leven had given her. It was as though she was the biggest mistake he had ever made. What made it worse was mere seconds earlier she was imagining him dropping to his knees and begging her to be his wife.

Selina looked up, realising she had been running without even thinking about the direction. The rain was persistent, although a little lighter than when they had first taken shelter, but there was a pervasive mist that obscured the trees and landmarks in the distance, meaning anything more than ten feet away looked hazy and out of focus.

They had been on the edge of the land belonging to Sir William and attached to Loch View Lodge. Selina had made her way to the road and was now still on it, but she wondered if she was heading in the wrong direction, going away from the house rather than towards it. She spun round, trying to find something that would allow her to pinpoint exactly where she was, but everything looked the same. She could not even see the cottage she had fled from.

The sensible thing to do would be to stick to the road. It ran between the house and the village of Ballachulish and so if she kept walking on it she would arrive at one or the other, but Selina hesitated. All she wanted was a warm bath in front of a hot fire. She did not want to walk to the village only to have to turn around to go all the way back again.

Despite knowing her next move was foolish, Selina decided to do it anyway. After everything that had happened she did not want to be out in this weather for any longer than was necessary.

Choosing the direction she thought the house was in, she stepped off the road. There was a grassy path where the ground was flattened by people walking and she thought if she followed this it would bring her into the gardens of Loch View Lodge. She had seen the other end of the path on her exploration of the gardens one day and she was almost certain this was the right route. Pushing away the niggle of doubt, she pressed on.

After walking for ten minutes Selina was beginning to get nervous. The path had petered out to nothing a few minutes earlier but she had carried on, hoping in a little way it would start up again, but that had not happened. She still could not see the house and she was getting a sinking sensation that she had just done something very, very stupid.

Panic seized her and she wondered if anyone had ever died out here in these hills. She knew she was not far from the house, but with the visibility as poor as it was now she could be a hundred feet away and not know it.

She bit her lip, regarding the way ahead and the way she had come. Every time she stopped, she worried that she was turning a little and had a fear of walking in circles for hours on end.

Selina made a decision, turning to the right and heading for a large tree twenty feet away. It had big branches and a full canopy of leaves, which would provide some shelter at least. She would have to wait for the worst of the mist and rain to pass and then head back to the road then.

Selina shivered. She was soaked to the skin, her dress sticking to her and chafing with every move she made. As she slumped down against the tree trunk she felt the tears well up inside her and she let them fall on to her cheeks. Her emotions had always run close to the surface, bubbling up unbidden. She could not help but smile if she found something amusing and she found it hard to stop the tears when she was upset.

The tears were cathartic, allowing her to acknowledge the hurt she was feeling deep inside. She told herself it would not hurt for long. In a few weeks she would be heading south, never to set eyes on Catherine Kingsley or Lord Leven ever again. They would be welcome to their miserable life together. It was obvious they would be unhappy. Catherine loved the vitality of life in London—the whirl of the social calendar, the visits to the modiste and the gossip she could share with friends. Lord Leven was completely the opposite and she doubted he would ever have any desire to visit London, or even Edinburgh. His passion was the land, the wilderness of Scotland and the people who called this part of the world their home.

Selina closed her eyes, trying to control the shudders that were threatening to take hold of all of her, clenching her teeth together and willing her body to be still.

* * *

The door opened before Callum could even raise a hand to knock and a footman peered out, concern etched on his face.

'Where is Miss Shepherd?' he said, his tone a little demanding before he remembered who he was talking to and quickly added, 'My lord.'

'She has not returned to the house?' An icy hand of dread clutched at him. This was what he had been afraid of. For him the journey back to the house from Mrs Douglas's cottage had taken only ten minutes. He'd walked briskly and stuck to the paths he had known well, but for Miss Shepherd it would all look confusing in the mist.

Before the footman could answer Sir William emerged, a smile on his face.

'You made it. Catherine is in the drawing room. I have sent for the local doctor although I understand he lives some way away. She is comfortable, though.' Sir William clapped him on the back. 'I thanked your friend for bringing her back and invited him to stay for tea, but he was eager to be on his way.'

Callum wondered if it had been Bruce's horse on the road that had made Hamish stand to attention and bark when they were in Mrs Douglas's cottage, that fateful bark that had broken the spell woven between him and Miss Shepherd.

'Come on through,' Sir William said, the most effusive Callum had seen him. 'I expect you wish to dry out. I will send for someone to light a fire.'

'Miss Shepherd, is she back?'

Sir William frowned as he looked around the grand entrance hall. 'Was she not with you?'

'No, we got separated in the mist. It is bad weather out there.'

The footman stepped forward, his hands clasped together and his voice a little tremulous. 'She has not returned, Sir William.'

'Ah. I expect she'll be along shortly,' Sir William said. 'Peters, keep a watch on the drive. Come through, Lord Leven, my daughter is eager to see you.' Callum allowed himself to be ushered into the drawing room and was greeted by the sight of Miss Kingsley reclining on a sofa, her ankle propped up on a pillow. She looked cooler and more composed than the last time he had seen her an hour earlier, riding off on the back of Bruce's horse.

'I must thank you, my lord,' Miss Kingsley said as soon as he entered the room. 'Your assistance up that mountain was chivalric.'

It had been a small hill, hardly a mountain, but he didn't correct her. He was more concerned at their lack of worry about Miss Shepherd.

'Miss Shepherd is missing,' he said without any

preamble. 'We got separated in the mist and she has not yet found her way home.'

'Separated?' Miss Kingsley said sharply. 'Surely it is hard to get separated on the straight road home.'

'Miss Shepherd must have strayed from the path.'

'Fool,' Miss Kingsley muttered.

'Of course, we will arrange for some of the servants to search for her. I expect she will appear any minute, but it is better to be safe,' Sir William said. He moved without any sense of urgency and Callum had to fight the urge to grab hold of the older man's shoulders and shake him. Sir William disappeared into the hall for a few moments and there was the low rumble of voices as he issued instructions. 'The male servants are going to set off and scour the local area.'

'Why don't you sit?' Lady Kingsley said, motioning to a free armchair close to Miss Kingsley. 'I expect you will want to stay until you know Miss Shepherd is home safe and well.'

'It could be a good opportunity to discuss the details of Catherine's dowry,' Sir William said.

For a moment Callum was too shocked to speak. If he was being charitable, he would reason that the Kingsleys did not know the Highlands the way he did. The hills were treacherous to the uninitiated and there were dozens of ways Miss Shepherd could have hurt herself while trying to get home. He was shocked by their lack of concern for this young woman they had taken in to their family. She might not be a close relative, but they were responsible for her safety while she travelled with them. Despite this none of them seemed to really care.

'I will join the search,' he said, spinning on his heel before anyone had the chance to reply. He was outside before the footmen and groomsmen had got themselves organised and spent a few minutes explaining the general area he had last seen Miss Shepherd. The servants were a mixture of local lads brought in while the family were in residence and a few that had travelled from the Kingsleys' London household. He mainly addressed the local young men, knowing they would be much quicker at traversing the challenging terrain than the English.

Despite his burning need to be out searching for Miss Shepherd, he took an extra thirty seconds to ensure everyone understood how and when to check back. The last thing they needed was for someone else to go missing and for no one to realise.

Callum was thankful that the rain had almost stopped now. The mist seemed a bit lighter, too, and visibility had improved somewhat. The weather changed quickly here in the Highlands, going from sunshine to rain in a matter of minutes, but it could also change back quickly, too. Probably there wouldn't be a cloud in the sky in time for sunset.

He retraced his steps towards the cottage, pausing at the points he thought Miss Shepherd might have stepped from the road to check for any sign of her. His tracking skills were honed in the snowy and icy terrains of Canada, but many of the same principles applied here.

At a point where a grassy path left the road he paused, noting the flattened grass that looked as though someone had recently walked this way. Quickly he followed the path, keeping his eyes locked for further signs that someone might have passed through.

He spotted the pale blue of her dress first, an incongruous detail in the landscape he knew so well. It helped that the mist was lifting and the rain had slowed to a gentle drizzle. He felt a rush of relief to find her which was replaced by panic as he realised she was not moving.

Filled with guilt, he rushed towards her, kneeling down on the wet grass underneath the tree. He could see why she had chosen this spot—the tree provided a good amount of shelter and had a broad trunk which she had propped herself up against.

'Miss Shepherd,' he said, reaching out and taking her hand. Her eyes opened and she looked at him, her expression one of relief mixed with a slight emptiness.

'Lord Leven,' she said after a moment.

'Callum,' he corrected her, even though he knew it was inappropriate after everything they had shared.

She shivered and he realised her fingers were hot beneath his touch. She had been out for only a couple of hours, but already her body was responding to the chill she had contracted with a fever.

'Come, Miss Shepherd, we must get you home.'

'You'll take me home?' Her voice was raspy and thin and he thought there was a hint of a smile on her lips. As he tried to pull her to her feet she closed her eyes.

'You must help me, Miss Shepherd.'

She opened her eyes again and this time he saw she was a little more composed. With his help she managed to stand, leaning heavily on the tree trunk while she got her balance.

'My head,' she whispered. 'Everything is spinning.'

'We need to get you back to Taigh Blath. Sir William has already summoned the doctor for Miss Kingsley. Doctor Frederickson can check you over, too.'

She nodded, managing to focus on his face for a moment. For now at least she was willing to let him help her, although no doubt as soon as he had assisted her home she would decide she never wanted to see him again. He would not blame her. The kiss had been inexcusable, his reaction after was that of a blundering fool.

She staggered a little as she walked, but he managed to get her back to the path and towards the main road. They did not speak, he wanted her to conserve all her energy for walking, but equally he did not know what to say to her. How did you tell someone you were besotted with them, but despite that you were determined to marry someone else?

When they were within fifty feet of the road she began to lean on him a little more until he felt her legs buckle underneath her. She slid to the ground, shivering, her head falling to her knees. A hand on the skin at the back of her neck confirmed his worst fears. Miss Shepherd was in the grips of a fever and it was only getting worse.

For the second time that day Callum lifted a young woman into his arms. Miss Shepherd was petite and he managed to get into a decent rhythm with his walking and breathing. He was aware the quicker he got her back to Taigh Blath, the sooner someone could strip her sodden clothes from her body and tuck her into bed. A chill such as this could be a dangerous thing and he only hoped her body was strong enough to fight it.

He almost groaned in relief when the house came into view. It took another five minutes to reach the front door, but even there he did not dare set Miss Shepherd down. If he put her down, he was not sure that he would have the strength to pick her up again and he wanted to get her to her bed.

The door opened and he was surprised to find Sir William standing there, looking shocked.

'Is she hurt?'

'A chill from being caught in the rain. Is the doctor here?'

'Not yet. Can you take her upstairs?'

Even as his leg muscles burned and his biceps throbbed he nodded, starting up the stairway in the centre of the house. Lady Kingsley stood at the bottom of the stairs, a grim expression on her face. He expected her to follow, to be the one to organise a fire in Miss Shepherd's room and the removal of her sodden clothes, but she did not move. Sir William led the way and once Callum had finally set Miss Shepherd down on top of her bedcovers it was Sir William who called for a maid to light the fire and see to the shivering young woman.

As Callum went to move away Miss Shepherd opened her eyes, a faint smile on her lips. She muttered something unintelligible, the only word he caught was *kiss*.

'Hush,' he said, tenderly stroking the hair from her face. 'You're safe now.'

Sir William must have seen the interaction, but he did not comment on it, instead waiting for Callum to leave the room before closing the door behind him and leaving the maid to see to Miss Shepherd.

'Will you stay for some refreshment?' Sir William said as they descended the stairs. There was no hint of any concern for Miss Shepherd, despite the delirious state she had been in. Sir William was a cold man, but Callum wondered if there was something else in the older man's lack of worry. The animosity between Miss Kingsley and Miss Shepherd was odd, but stranger still was the contemptuous way Lady Kingsley treated the young woman they said was a distant relative. In the few brief interactions he had witnessed they had all treated Miss Shepherd as an inconvenience.

'No,' he said brusquely. 'I need to go home and change. I will call tomorrow to find out how Miss Shepherd and Miss Kingsley fare.'

Sir William inclined his head, deciding not to

push the matter and Callum stalked from the house, calling Hamish to heel, his thoughts still with Miss Shepherd.

Chapter Ten

'Don't gawp, you look like a fish,' Catherine said as she gave Selina a scornful look.

'This isn't the first dance I have been to.'

'I hardly think your provincial little gatherings in the local assembly rooms can be compared to a celebration such as this.'

Selina didn't like to point that *this* was nothing more than a provincial gathering in a local assembly room. Sir William had agreed to a very generous budget and Lady Kingsley and Catherine had spent the best part of the week bargaining and cajoling the locals into providing everything that was needed for a ball despite it being held in the small village hall in Ballachulish. The result was the aesthetic of a grand ball, but in a tiny, rustic space.

'Try not to embarrass yourself tonight,' Catherine continued. 'Wait to be introduced before speaking to people. If anyone deigns to ask you to dance, then accept graciously...' she paused, giving Selina an assessing look '...or perhaps it is better if you decline graciously.'

'I'm not going to embarrass myself or you,' Selina said, wishing she could slip away into the gathering crowd already.

'This is important,' Catherine said forcefully. 'You may not care if I marry Lord Leven, but I am determined this match will be settled in the coming few days. I will be married and I will be a countess—' she lowered her voice so no one but Selina could hear '—even if it means I'm a countess of a horrible little place like this.'

The room was already hot with the press of bodies inside. One of the housemaids, a local girl who had been hired to work for the Kingsleys while they were at Loch View Lodge, had told Selina that there hadn't been a dance in Ballachulish for well over a decade. It was a small community and many of the young people had left to find opportunities for work elsewhere. There was not much in the way of high Society and the housemaid had been excited to tell Selina that half the village had been invited to make up numbers. The young women were wearing their best church dresses and the men their smartly pressed kilts.

'I think Ballachulish is a delightful village,' Selina said.

Catherine snorted, earning her an admonishing look from Lady Kingsley.

'Selina, step back,' Lady Kingsley said sharply. 'No one needs to see you. This is Catherine's moment.'

Selina rolled her eyes and stepped back. The last few days had been pure misery while she was stuck indoors with the Kingsleys. The doctor who had visited after she had contracted a chill had advised she stay inside even after her fever broke and she began to feel stronger. It had meant countless hours spent wandering Loch View Lodge, trying to avoid any of the Kingsleys, but all too often she had been forced into their company.

Thankfully no one had protested to her slipping away when Lord Leven came to visit and no one had questioned why. When Sir William had asked if she had maintained her end of their bargain in helping to show Catherine's good side she had merely replied that Lord Leven was eager to proceed with the marriage. It was not a lie and her father seemed satisfied with the outcome.

Surreptitiously she eyed the crowd, hating how her pulse quickened when Lord Leven stepped forward to greet them. She was surprised to see him in trousers, one of the only men there without a kilt. His eyes sought her out, but she steadfastly refused to meet them and once he was distracted by Catherine she went to step away, surprised when her father caught her arm.

'Lord Leven was asking after you yesterday. Remember our agreement. Talk to him tonight, make him see he must agree to my terms.'

Selina nodded, not daring to pull her arm away, but hating how she felt used by him. It was impossible to imagine how she could ever have believed that one day he might come to care for her. Sir William was a cold-hearted man and Selina wasn't even sure he loved his legitimate daughter. He certainly didn't appear to consider Catherine's feelings about the marriage—she didn't think the young woman had been consulted once.

Luckily Catherine seemed as determined as her father to marry Lord Leven, her ambitions allowing her to overlook all the downsides of the match as long as she ended up titled. There was no way her father was ever going to see Selina as anything more than an inconvenience, a dirty little secret that he had to keep close by to ensure she did not jeopardise his chance of climbing higher in the Society he wanted to be a part of so much.

Instead of disappearing into the crowd as she'd

planned, Selina stepped forward, flashing her widest smile at Lord Leven. After a few seconds her cheeks hurt at the unnatural expression and she wondered if it looked more like a grimace than anything else.

'Lord Leven, I wanted to thank you for coming to my rescue last week,' she said.

He inclined his head, narrowing his eyes. For a whole week she had avoided him, disappearing to her room whenever he came to visit. He would wonder why she was keen to speak to him now.

'I am pleased to see you fully recovered, Miss Shepherd.'

'I cannot wait for the dancing later this evening,' Catherine said as Selina came to stand beside her, her shoulders rising up as if she were readying for a fight.

'I was just about to go and fetch Miss Kingsley a glass of lemonade,' he said, motioning to a table set to one side of the room. 'Perhaps you would like a glass.'

'Wonderful,' Selina said, linking her hand through his arm even though he had not offered it to her. 'I shall come with you.'

'Selina,' Catherine said, displeasure evident on her face.

'Do not fear, I will return Lord Leven to you in time for your dance.'

For a moment Lord Leven did not move, surprised by her sudden assertiveness and her willingness to talk to him after a week of avoiding him. Selina had to pull on his arm to get him to step away.

'You are talking to me, then,' Lord Leven murmured, his voice sending an involuntary shiver down Selina's spine. She silently cursed her own foolishness, wondering how her subconscious could still desire Lord Leven after the horrific rejection she had suffered at his hands.

'Barely,' Selina said, the rictus smile still fixed on her face. 'But you are my ticket home and I have decided I will do anything to get away from the Kingsleys.'

'And that involves pretending to talk to me?'

She sighed, turning to him, the irritation swirling inside her. She hated that her eyes lingered on his lips, remembering how it had felt when he had kissed her and her body swayed closer to his, wanting one elusive touch.

'Sir William wants you to marry Catherine and he will do anything to get an advantage over you so you accept his terms. That includes using me to sing Catherine's praises, despite me really thinking she is akin to a demon sent from hell itself.'

'You would not be my choice of advocate for her,' Lord Leven murmured.

'Luckily I do not have to do anything because you want to marry Catherine as much as Sir William wants you to marry her. So I can be here pretending to talk to you about Catherine Kingsley, then one day soon you will ask for her hand in marriage and everyone will think I helped the proposal go ahead. I get my ticket home and never have to set eyes on the Kingsleys or you ever again.'

'A foolproof plan.'

'It is,' Selina said, reaching out for a glass of lemonade and taking a huge gulp. The liquid was sharp, much sharper than she had anticipated and it caught in the back of her throat, making her cough.

Lord Leven took the glass from her and set it down on the table.

'Steady.'

Selina caught her breath and picked up the glass again, looking Lord Leven in the eye as she took another gulp.

'Now we pretend to talk for a few minutes and then you return to Miss Kingsley and are effusive towards her. You can mention something complimentary I said about her.'

'Perhaps the observation she is like a demon sent from hell.'

'This is not a laughing matter, my lord.'

Lord Leven schooled his face into a serious expression. 'What shall we pretend to talk about?'

Selina sighed. 'I do not care.'

'Perhaps the wonders of astronomy and the recent alignment of the planets? Or the trials and tribulations of James Cook on his adventure around the globe.'

Selina turned to him, desperately trying to control herself. 'You might find this amusing, my lord, but I do not.'

He puffed out his cheeks and exhaled. 'Perhaps a dance would help.'

'It would not.'

'No, no, no,' he said, taking the glass of lemonade from her hand again. 'I think this is the best idea.'

'I said no.' She wrenched her arm away from him and then remembered herself. The room was crowded, but people's eyes would be on them. Lord Leven was an important man in Ballachulish.

He shrugged. 'What about a walk around the perimeter of the ballroom? It might look a little more natural than us standing here with you glaring at me.'

'I'm not glaring.'

For a moment he bent his knees so his eyes were level with hers. 'I have received many a glare in my time and you, Miss Shepherd, are glaring.'

She let out a little, irritated huff and turned away, struggling to keep control. Once she felt some of the anger melt away she turned back. 'Perhaps I am,' she said, a little calmer, 'but I think I have good reason to glare, do you not agree?'

Lord Leven suddenly turned serious.

'Of course,' he murmured. 'I want to apologise again for my behaviour last week. It was unforgivable.'

Selina closed her eyes. She did not want his apology. All she wanted was to get far from here and never have to see Lord Leven again.

They fell silent, standing together awkwardly until Selina caught Lady Kingsley craning her neck and looking in their direction.

'I think you are wanted by the Kingsleys. I suggest you take Miss Kingsley her lemonade.' Before Lord Leven could say anything more she stepped away, thankful for the crowd.

'Miss Shepherd,' a booming voice called out and Selina turned to see the giant form of Mr Bruce. 'I hear you had quite an adventure after I left you last week. I am glad to see you recovered.' He took her hand and pumped it hard up and down as if they were two businessmen settling on an agreeable deal.

'Thank you. And thank you for assisting Miss Kingsley last week.'

'It was my pleasure. Always glad to help a friend. Ah, can you hear the music? I think it is time for a dance. Will you step with me?'

'You want to dance with me?'

He shrugged. 'I may look like a bear, but I dance with the grace of a doe.'

Selina smiled, feeling her spirits lift a little for the first time in days.

'A doe, you say...'

'You're tempted, admit it, Miss Shepherd. Come, I promise not to step on your toes.'

He led her to the dance floor, joining dozens of other couples as the music started in earnest. It was not a tune she recognised and she was glad when Mr Bruce leaned in close and told her just to copy him. 'No one here cares how anyone else dances. It is just about having fun.'

All evening Callum had struggled to stay present in the moment. His eyes constantly roamed across the room, hoping to catch a glimpse of Miss Shepherd. He knew this obsession with searching her out was unhealthy, but he could not help himself. For the first hour he had dedicated himself to Miss Kingsley, hating every moment he stood stiffly by her side. They had nothing to talk about, no shared interests. She was constantly on edge, trying to impress him with her grace and elegance without realising they were not qualities he was searching for.

Now he had made his excuses, telling the Kingsleys he needed to spend some time with the other guests. In truth, he had retreated to a corner and watched Miss Shepherd.

'Your expression could scare a warrior,' his mother said as she emerged from the crowd, cheeks pink and her dress crumpled from the dancing.

'Good evening, Mother.'

'I've been watching you this past half an hour,' she said, coming to stand beside him. 'And it is not your future wife you have not been able to take your eyes off.'

Callum hated that his distress was so obvious. He prided himself on being a stoic, unreadable person, his emotions kept hidden.

'The young lady you can't keep your eyes off is a pretty little thing.'

Callum didn't say anything. His mother could have a job as royal inquisitor in the Tower of London, but he had learned over the years how best to withstand her probing.

'She is connected to the Kingsleys, I believe. The official story is she is some distant relative—you know how the English like to pretend they are charitable by taking in destitute relatives and having them fulfil some odd role halfway between family member and servant.'

'That is not the truth?'

Lady Leven shrugged. 'Take a look at Sir William. He is a fine-looking man for someone of his age. A full head of brown hair, good cheekbones, clear skin. In his youth I expect he was popular among the young women. Now look at Miss Shepherd. There is a certain resemblance, is there not?'

'They do proclaim her to be a relative, if somewhat distant.'

'What do I know, my dear? I am just a foolish old woman who has too much time on her hands and a penchant for intrigue.'

'You think Miss Shepherd is his daughter?'

'I do. I think he got some poor young woman pregnant years ago and Miss Shepherd was the result. What I cannot fathom is why he has brought her here to Scotland with him. High Society is full of wealthy men hiding their illegitimate children, some are more open about things than others, but Sir William shows no affection towards Miss Shepherd, so why is she here?'

Callum thought of her enthusiasm for life, of the way she threw herself into everything. He did not know for certain his mother was right about Miss Shepherd's origins, but it would explain some of the odd dynamic within the Kingsley household. Lady Kingsley found it hard to hide her disdain for Miss Shepherd, which was a little more understandable if she was Sir William's illegitimate daughter than if she was merely a poor relation. It also explained some of the rivalry between Miss Kingsley and Miss Shepherd.

His eyes fixed back on to Miss Shepherd as she spoke with Mr Bruce and Miss Scott. Bruce had swooped in and brought her into the heart of the dance, introducing her to all the locals, leaving her to dance with the men of the village, only to pick her back up once the dancing was done and guide her to the next group. He was a good man, a good friend.

'She is keen to get back to England.'

Lady Leven regarded him with sadness in her eyes. 'You look at her as if you were starved, my dear. Yet on the few occasions you have looked at Miss Kingsley there is only pain and panic in your eyes.' She held up her hands to ward off his protests. 'I know you are doing it for the family, for the locals. It is a very selfless thing to do, but no one wishes to see you unhappy.'

'I know,' he said softly. No one wished to see him unhappy, but that did not mean he could abandon them and selfishly indulge his own desires instead. That would make him no better than his father.

'Perhaps you could dance with Miss Shepherd. One dance would not hurt.'

'She will not dance with me.'

'Ah. Something has happened between you.'

Callum closed his eyes, remembering as he had a thousand times in the last week their kiss in old Mrs Douglas's cottage. He had relived the kiss again and again, fearful he might forget what her lips tasted of or how her skin had felt underneath his fingers. It was ridiculous, to think of something that could never be repeated so often, to live through it again and again.

'I expect she'll forgive you if you showed her why you're doing all this.'

'I have told her. She knows I must choose my duty.'

His mother looked at him with a raised eyebrow. 'I hope you were not as blunt as all that.'

'There is no other way to say it.'

'Good lord, Callum, did I really raise such an insensitive fool? You want her forgiveness, I take it, for some…transgression?'

He grimaced. Sometimes it was highly irritating having such an astute woman as his mother. It was hard to hide anything from her.

'Aye.'

'And you have apologised?'

'Aye.'

'Then you need to show her why you cannot follow your desires. Don't just tell her, show her the people you are doing this for, the land you are trying to restore.'

'That is a little hard if she will not speak to me.'

'I did not only see how you looked at her. I saw how she looked at you, Callum. You are a difficult devil to resist.'

She squeezed his arm affectionately and then turned away, disappearing into the crowd and leaving him with his thoughts once again. After a few seconds he found his eyes roaming the room, searching for Miss Shepherd, the sense of alarm building when he could not see her or Mr Bruce anywhere.

Chapter Eleven

'If I ask you a question, do you promise to tell me the truth?' Selina said, looking up at the bear of a man beside her. Mr Bruce had been a perfect companion all evening, introducing her to dozens of people, organising her dance card as if he were an ambitious mother seeking out the best suitors. He had ensured she always had a drink in her hand and a smile on her face. Never had she expected this evening to be anything other than an ordeal, but she had enjoyed almost every minute of it.

'Of course.'

'Did Lord Leven ask you to watch over me?'

Bruce puffed out his cheeks and shook his head. 'There's not getting much past you, is there?' He must have seen her expression for he rushed to reassure her. 'Not that it wasn't a wonderful evening. I have not had that much fun in a decade.'

'I did enjoy myself,' she said, smiling, but finding it difficult to banish the disappointment.

'Callum is a little rough around the edges. Any man who lives that long on his own with just a dog for company, they lose a little of their refinement, but he is a good man, a kind man. I do not know what passed between you, but he told me you would not wish to spend the evening with him, but he did not want you to be left standing in the corner.'

'He thinks I am incapable of speaking to people without someone to guide me.'

'We can be an intimidating lot. Everyone knows one another but you.'

Selina had to concede he was right. Without Mr Bruce guiding her through the evening, she would have likely spent her time wishing away the hours and wondering when she could make her escape.

'Do you wish to go home? I can arrange for someone to take you back to Taigh Blath if you would rather.'

It did not take long to make her decision. Her evening might have been carefully choreographed by Lord Leven, but that did not mean she had to cut short her enjoyment just to spite him.

'You promised me a proper Scottish celebration,' Selina said, eliciting a huge grin from Mr Bruce.

'That I did, follow me.'

It was dark outside and Selina was aware she should probably not step out into the unknown with a man she had met only once before, but she had drunk three glasses of strong wine over the course of the evening and she was feeling reckless. Besides, Mr Bruce had been nothing but a gentleman all night, never once glancing at her in a predatory manner.

They walked from the village hall, which had half-emptied of people now, to another building that was on the outskirts of the settlement. In the darkness Selina couldn't be completely sure, but she thought it might be a barn. Light spilled out from within and there was the sound of lively music and the hum of dozens of people talking and laughing.

As she opened the door Selina felt a rush of warmth and happiness. The dance in the village hall had been fun, but there was a sense everyone was holding back, aware they were to make a good impression on the man who owned most of the property in the local area. Here there were no restrictions, no one watching over them and judging.

'Miss Shepherd,' a young woman called out on seeing Selina. 'Come join us. We are gossiping about all the fine young men in Ballachulish and we need a newcomer's point of view.'

Selina allowed herself happily to be swept into their fold, feeling a glow of happiness and belonging that she hadn't for a long time. The past year living with the Kingsleys had been difficult, but until recently she had struggled to see how unhappy it was making her. Convinced that with a little time Sir William would see her worth, Selina had felt a little bit more of a failure every day he treated her barely any better than the housemaids in his employ. It had eaten away at her self-esteem and made it even harder for her to realise she needed to leave.

Here, with the young women of the remote Scottish village, she was reminded how it felt to be surrounded by people who didn't actively want you to disappear. Every day was a battle to stay out of Catherine's way and to ensure she did nothing to anger Lady Kingsley. Every word she said had to be carefully chosen, every action scrutinised and judged.

The feeling reinforced her determination to finally give up on the idea of Sir William as a loving father, as a man who wanted to provide even his illegitimate daughter with a good start in life. He had shown her his true character right from the very start, but until now she had refused to believe him. Now she had accepted he was an uncaring, selfish, social climber, she could look at the whole situation much more objectively.

'I cannot wait for your brother to come home,

Agnes,' one of the young women was saying. 'He has the nicest smile in all the Highlands.'

'Hands off our Robert,' Agnes said laughing. 'Poor man hasn't even set foot back in Scotland yet and you're all set to scare him off.'

'Your brother has been away?' Selina asked the young woman beside her.

'Working in Newcastle for the last three years. He's only been home once in that time when our dad died.'

'All three of my brothers have left,' another young woman said. 'Two went voluntarily on the ships, another moved to a fishing village on the coast, but he's no fisherman. I doubt it will be long before he goes overseas as well.'

'Why have they left?' Selina asked and all the faces in the little group turned to her.

'There is no work here, not since the estate was sold. Rents are going up and Sir William does not want tenants farming his land. He makes much more profit with sheep.'

Another woman spoke, her voice quiet but filled with passion. 'Sir William is no fool, he does not want the unrest many other landlords have had with the forced evictions, but he can get the same result by not providing work for our men and by not renewing the leases on our houses when they come up.'

For a moment there was silence and then Agnes

rallied. 'Enough of this maudlin talk. Tonight is a celebration. Soon Lord Leven will be in charge and our fortunes will be changing.'

'And your brother will be coming home,' one of the women said to shouts of laughter from her friends.

'Can I ask you a question?' Selina said, leaning in so they couldn't be overheard. 'Why does Lord Leven not wear a kilt? Many of the men here do...'

'He used to,' one young woman volunteered. 'Even as a young lad he had good legs.'

'Imagine him in a kilt now,' another woman said, flushing red in the cheeks.

'The rumour is that ever since losing his ancestral lands he does not feel worthy to wear the family tartan,' Agnes said.

The door behind them opened and Lord Leven walked in. There was a momentary pause in conversation until he shut the door behind him and called out, 'If someone doesn't pick up their violin and play a tune in the next ten seconds, I'll be up at the front myself and you'll all have to put up with the screeching of my bow.'

There was a roar of laughter and the music started again, as did the chatter.

The young women around Selina seemed to melt away as Lord Leven approached, all flushing and giggling as the handsome lord greeted them with a smile. When he turned to Selina his expression was serious.

'I see that reprobate Bruce brought you to the real party.'

'He did,' Selina said. The ire she had felt towards the man earlier in the evening had dissipated somewhat and she did not immediately turn to go. 'I told the Kingsleys I was going back to Loch View Lodge—Taigh Blath,' she corrected herself. 'I doubt they would even think to check I got back safely.'

'I should insist you go home…'

'But you won't.'

He looked at her for a long moment and then smiled softly. 'You have one hour, Miss Shepherd, then I will see you home myself.'

'I know you asked Mr Bruce to ensure I had a good time this evening,' Selina said. Lord Leven's eyes were searching her face, trying to work out why she had lost the fierce animosity she had harboured towards him earlier in the evening.

'I did not want it to be a terrible evening for you and I was aware you likely would not wish for my company.'

'And you needed to be with Miss Kingsley.'

He didn't answer for a moment. 'And I needed to be with Miss Kingsley,' he agreed eventually.

'It worked,' Selina said.

He raised an eyebrow.

'I had a good time. Despite being completely and utterly convinced I would not, I enjoyed myself more than I ever have at a social event.'

'High praise indeed. Bruce could make even a wake entertaining.' He paused, seeming to consider whether to say what he was thinking next. 'Indulge me, Miss Shepherd. The last time we spoke you looked at me as if you wished someone would boil me in a cauldron of hot oil.'

'That isn't quite true,' she said, allowing herself a little smile. 'I looked at you as if *I* wished to boil you in a cauldron of hot oil.'

'Why the change of heart?'

'You are very direct, has anyone ever told you that?'

'You forget I have never been part of gentle London Society.'

'Nonsense. Nor have I and I know the civilised way to do things is to skirt around a question, asking it in a dozen different ways except the one that will actually get you a direct answer.'

He shrugged. 'I think my way is better.'

Selina sighed, looking around the room for a moment. 'I was hurt. I *am* hurt. Do you know how humiliating it is for your first kiss to be followed by such a look of revulsion and horror that you wondered if you sprouted a deforming facial growth halfway through it?'

'Not revulsion,' Lord Leven said quickly.

'Certainly horror.'

He did not deny this one and Selina had to push away the prickle of hurt that threatened to take hold.

'I admit I did not handle things well.'

'I was hurt and that was all I could think about, but this evening do you know what I have heard over and over?'

He shook his head.

'Praise for you, some outright, some abstract, but these people hail you as their saviour.'

A shadow crossed his face and Selina realised what a burden this must be for the Earl. To have an extended group of people relying on you to restore their fortunes. It was more than one man should have to bear.

'I am no saviour.'

'But you are working to make life a little better for them.'

'They are my responsibility.'

'No man should be responsible for the future of so many.'

'Yet that is the way the world works. If Sir William holds on to the estate, how long is it before he realises the model of small farms run by tenant farmers is not all that profitable? Just like all the other landowners he will turn the people off, refuse to renew their leases when the current ones come to an end. Then where will they be?

'Forced to move south or to the harsh fishing communities on the coast, or perhaps even abroad. Families will be split, with the most able going where the work is and the old and infirm or the very young left behind. We will lose everything that made Ballachulish a good place to live.'

'I understand a lot have left already.'

'They have. To find work elsewhere, but I hope one day we can tempt them back.'

Selina nodded. 'I'm not saying I entirely forgive you,' she said, a little smile tugging at her lips, 'But I realise I was a little selfish. I was thinking of me and you, not everyone else your actions affect.'

'Thank you.'

'And I will not do anything to jeopardise your arrangement with the Kingsleys.'

'I am grateful for your understanding. We shall be friends.'

'Yes, friends.'

'And a friend never refuses another friend a dance.'

As if on cue the music picked up its pace and Lord Leven held out his hand, tilting his head towards her in question.

'I do not know the steps.'

'I promise I will not let you fall.'

Selina bit her lip. She loved to dance and already the music was pulsing through her, enticing her to the dance floor.

'I can see you are tempted. Let me show you the true pleasure of a Scottish dance.'

She could not refuse him, not when his eyes twinkled in such a manner and his smile drew her in. Selina caught herself, desperate not to fall for him all over again. *Friends*, she told herself, that was all they could be.

With butterflies in her stomach she placed her hand into Lord Leven's and followed him to the dance floor.

'Can you feel the beat? I always imagine this part to be played by the drummers in a regiment, spurring everyone on.'

'This is a battle song?'

'No, you'd know if it were a battle song. We're seventy years since Culloden, but there are men here who learned the war songs from their fathers and grandfathers. They would be on their feet, stamping and cheering and singing every word. If you stay late, you might get to witness one or two of those, they normally only come out when everyone is good and drunk.'

'Will you be good and drunk, my lord?'

He gave her a mischievous grin that made him look younger and more carefree and shrugged.

'It would be rude not to. I don't want the people thinking I'm aloof and distant and there is no greater equaliser than copious amounts of free-flowing alcohol.'

'I will be sorry to miss that spectacle, then.'

They were in the very middle of the dance floor, lined up with a dozen other couples all in high spirits. The music was fast and Selina had the sense that she was about to get lost in the middle of the crowd.

She had been dancing the fast-paced Scottish dances all evening and had worked out the best thing to do was to hold her partner's hand and allow herself to be swept away, not caring if she did not do the right steps at the right time. No one noticed and no one cared, as long as spirits were high and the music loud.

Unsurprisingly, Callum danced well. She had seen him move effortlessly through the Scottish countryside, covering huge distances without even breaking a sweat. He had climbed the steep hill from the loch as if it were the gentlest of slopes and pulled himself up into the tree beside her a couple of weeks earlier without having to strain. He was a physically fit man, nimble on his feet, and tonight she had caught glimpses of the advantages of his upbringing.

He was at home among these people, his friends and his neighbours, but he stood out. His speech was a little more refined, his mannerisms and posture had been coached and corrected from a young age. It was apparent in how he danced, too. He threw himself into the steps as much as anyone else there, but he managed to do so without a hair coming out of place or his shirt looking ruffled.

Selina found it hard to tear her eyes away from him, even at the point in the dance where they swapped partners for a moment. She yearned for his hand on her waist again, for the heat of his body close to hers.

As the music slowed and faded Callum reached out and took her hand, kissing the skin below her knuckles lightly. She felt disappointed that the dance was over, knowing Callum, with his rigid self-control, would not risk another with her.

'Do not step away from the dance floor,' the young man who had been playing the violin called, his eyes seemingly fixed on Callum. Bruce was standing close to him, just off the raised platform that had hastily been constructed for the small group of musicians, and he caught Selina's eye, winking at her. 'Grab hold of your partner and hold them close.'

For a moment Selina wondered if Callum would

walk away. It was the sensible thing to do. They had both shown they could not be trusted with one another. Desire, lust, yearning—whatever you wanted to call the spark that crackled and burned between them, it was not sensible to fuel it, but to her surprise he held out his hand.

He drew her close, mirroring the actions of the other couples on the makeshift dance floor, and together they began to move to the music. It was a haunting piece, the notes low and drawn out, and as they danced Selina did not dare look up at Callum, too scared of what he might see in her eyes.

She was lonely, terribly so. Lonely and scared, not knowing what her future held. She knew she had to be strong, to step out and find her own path in life, but the idea was daunting. Always she had been one of a pair, her twin sister, so different in temperament but such a big part of her life.

'You look sad, Miss Shepherd.'

'Selina,' she said, looking up at him with a soft smile. 'If we are to be friends, you should call me Selina.'

Callum inhaled sharply and she felt his fingers flex slightly through the thin material of her dress.

'Selina,' he murmured.

'I'm not sad,' she said eventually. 'I was thinking this has been one of the best nights of my life.'

She glanced up at him, their eyes meeting. For a long moment Callum did not speak. When he did, his voice was gruff, as if the emotion was catching in his throat. 'You could stay.'

'Stay here? In Ballachulish.'

'Why not?'

Selina shook her head. 'No. You would be married to Catherine and I would…' She trailed off, not wanting to think of how hard it would be to see Callum from a distance, living a life she could never truly be a part of.

As the music finished and the couples slowly moved apart, Callum didn't relinquish his hold on Selina for a moment longer. He looked down at her, studying her face. 'I don't want this to be the only time we dance.'

Selina felt her heart wrench inside her chest and realised he felt it too. The deeper connection, the yearning. It was more than desire, more than a base, animal attraction, although that was there, too. She couldn't call it love—no sane person could believe they had fallen in love with a man they had only known two weeks—but there was something deeper, something that threatened to overpower and take away all logic.

Summoning a smile, she tilted her chin back and met his eye. 'I am sure no one could object to us sharing a dance at your wedding celebrations.' For a moment Selina wasn't sure if she had pushed Calum too far, but after ten seconds of tense silence he threw his head back and laughed.

'Maybe you're right. Come on, I need a stiff drink.' He took her hand, the gesture too intimate, but Selina could not bring herself to pull away. She reasoned everyone else was too engrossed in their own affairs to notice Lord Leven holding her hand.

Chapter Twelve

'I think it might be time to escort Miss Shepherd home,' Lady Leven said, touching Callum's arm lightly. It was the early hours of the morning and, although the barn was still half-full, a lot of the locals had drifted away in the last half an hour, seeking out the comfort of their beds.

Selina was seated on an upturned box, surrounded by some of the young women of the area. She had an easy manner about her and made friends quickly and the local women had swept her into their group whenever he had stepped away.

'I know that family of hers are neglectful, but you do not want to be caught trying to sneak her back into Taigh Blath as the household begins to wake up.'

He nodded. His mother was right. In truth, he should have seen that Miss Shepherd was safely home hours earlier, but he had been caught up in the revelry of the evening and enjoyed spending time with her too much, away from the ever-watchful eyes of the Kingsleys.

'What about you? Will you stay here until I return so I can escort you home?'

His mother gave him an admonishing look. 'If I cannot walk back home by myself safely in the village where I have lived these last thirty years I do not know what the world is coming to.'

'A lot of people have had far too much to drink…'

'You fuss too much.'

'Let me at least ask Bruce to see you home. You know he would see it as an honour.'

For a moment he thought she would refuse, but after surveying his face, a soft smile on her lips, she nodded. 'Very well.'

It only took a minute to ask the favour of his old friend and Bruce agreed immediately. Callum thanked the big bear of a man and then turned his attention back to Selina.

'Can I walk you home?' he asked quietly, leaning in to speak the words into her ear so only she could hear.

Selina turned quickly, her chin lifting so her face was only inches away from his. Her cheeks were flushed and her hair a little dishevelled, a testament to the raucous nature of the dance in hours past.

Wordlessly she nodded, rising up from her seat on

the upturned box before turning her attention back to the women she had been talking to.

One by one they embraced her, gushing about what a wonderful night they'd all had. Callum marvelled at how easily Selina had fit in to their tight-knit community. Newcomers were normally viewed with suspicion, especially newcomers from south of the border, but Selina, with her easy manner, had been accepted immediately.

For a moment he allowed himself to imagine what it would be like to marry Selina instead of Catherine Kingsley. He knew the community would take a long time to accept Catherine, even if all the while they were happy that he had found a way to restore the lands that had been sold off as part of his father's debts. Everyone would be wary of the daughter of Sir William, the man who had taken so much from them.

In the end he had to pull Selina away from her new friends, earning him a chorus of moans. Thankfully once she was holding on to his arm Callum was able to guide Selina out of the barn quickly.

Outside Selina gasped and for a second he thought something was wrong. He felt a sense of trepidation surge through his veins and immediately he was on high alert, but then he caught a glimpse of her face. She had tipped her head back and was staring up at the stars.

'They're the same here,' she whispered.

'The same as down south?'

She nodded, her eyes fixed on the sky above.

'Aye, they are.'

'It makes the world feel a little bit smaller, doesn't it, thinking we're all looking at the same sky.'

He came to stand half beside her, half behind her, and gently picked up her hand and placed it so it rested on his. At first she stiffened, but the alcohol had made her less wary and after a moment she relaxed into him. Slowly he guided her hand, tracing out the patterns the stars made in the darkness.

'There is Orion, with his shield held high, and over there is Centaurus, with the torso and head of a man and the body and legs of a horse. And right here are my two favourite constellations, Ursa Major and Ursa Minor.'

'The bears?'

'Aye. I always like to think of them as a mother and her cub.'

'How do you remember where all the different constellations are?' she asked, her voice filled with wonder. She swayed back towards him as she spoke, her head brushing against his shoulder.

'There wasn't much else to do on the long nights in the Canadian wilderness.'

'You spent your nights outside?'

'Some of them.'

'Someone must have taught you.'

'There were a group of us. All travelling the same area, although not strictly working together. Of a night time we would gather in the tavern of whatever little town we were passing through, or if it was a night spent in the wilderness we would share a campfire. Many of those men were Scottish and only too happy to share their wisdom with a naive young lad like me.'

'What was it you did when you were out there?'

'I worked with animals, horses mainly but sometimes beasts of burden. The company I worked for sold the horses and I would deliver them to where they needed to be—often far out into the wilderness.'

'You went off on your own on these expeditions?'

'Until I rescued Hamish. As I say, there were other people following the same roads: fur traders, merchants and men looking for work.'

'It sounds a very lonely life.'

Callum looked down at her as she turned and their eyes met and he found himself nodding. The loneliness wasn't something he liked to admit to. He'd gone from a community that was close, where everyone knew his name, to sometimes spending a week with only his dog for company.

'It was worth it in the end. I made myself useful,

eventually saved up enough to become a partner in the company. After many years I made enough to return home with a good amount of money saved up.'

Selina smiled at him sadly. 'It is not weakness to admit you were lonely. Just as it is not weakness to admit you want something different from the future you are forcing yourself into.'

'Say what you really feel, Selina,' he murmured, a smile on his lips.

'Would you prefer I lied to you?' Her expression was earnest despite the slight running together of her words.

'No.'

For a long moment neither of them moved. Selina's eyes searched his face with an intensity he had never felt before and he had the horrible, crushing sensation that she might find him wanting.

'We need to get you home,' he said eventually, her scrutiny becoming too much for him. She didn't move. He turned back to face her. They were still only fifty feet away from the barn and the sound of the music starting up again floated out.

'Did you think this was how your life would be?' she asked.

'If I answer you, will you allow me to escort you home?'

'I will.'

'No.'

'That is all you are going to give me?'

He offered her his arm and this time she took it, moving so her body was close to his. The night was relatively warm, but it was well after midnight and there was a little chill to the air.

'You want to know what I was like as an idealistic eighteen-year-old.'

'More than anything in the world.'

He glanced over at her and found himself getting swept away by her infectious good spirits.

'Fine. I will reveal my adolescent hopes and dreams, but only if you do the same.'

'Eighteen was only a few years ago for me.'

'I feel as though you are implying I am old.'

She shrugged, grinning mischievously again. There was something of the carefree young woman about her tonight and Callum realised he was getting a glimpse of the woman who had existed before the Kingsleys had subdued and suppressed her. From their conversations he knew a little about her life, of the time she had spent as a girl growing up on the Sussex coast, to the year she had spent in London with the Kingsleys before travelling up here with them to Scotland. She had spoken fondly of a sister, a twin if he remembered correctly. Someone she missed dearly.

'When I was a lad I knew one thing with such burning certainty that sometimes it hurt. I knew whatever happened I did not want to turn into my father.'

'He wasn't a good father?'

'No.' Callum shrugged, half-acknowledging he was judging the man harshly. During the early years of his childhood there had been good times, before the drink had become more important to his father than anything else, but those memories were distant, overshadowed by what had come next.

'He had these dark moods, fuelled by alcohol. Sometimes he would sink into a deep melancholy for weeks on end and barely rise from bed. Other times he was up and functioning, but quick to anger. Even the slightest hint of criticism would set him off. He was like an unruly toddler, consumed by anger. He'd throw things at the staff—once I can remember my mother being particularly concerned about a maid who'd had a full pot of ink thrown at her head.'

'That's awful.'

Callum couldn't bring himself to look at Selina. He hated pity, hated being seen as vulnerable. Normally he didn't like to talk about his childhood—if anyone asked he would just shrug and say it was fine. Selina had a way of making him relax his guard and often he would find himself revealing things he otherwise wouldn't ever think of telling someone.

'Not as awful as many. I had a loving mother, a safe home, enough food and a good education. Compared to the childhoods of many children...'

She spun to face him and interrupted with a firm shake of her head. 'No, you don't have to do that.'

'Do what?'

'Rationalise something that is so emotional. Just because you were not beaten and starving in a gutter, it does not mean you cannot be affected by the things that have happened to you.' She took a breath and then carried on before he could say anything in reply. 'Take my childhood. To most people looking in it was happy.' She grimaced and shook her head. 'Most of the time it *was* happy. I had a loving mother and a sister to share everything with. We were far from wealthy, but we never starved and always had a roof over our heads.'

Callum said nothing, wondering if she was going to continue. Until now she'd been vague about her past, telling him with great enthusiasm about the beauty of the Sussex town she grew up in, the walks along the cliffs and the evenings spent watching the crashing waves from their house up on the hill.

She'd spoken of her sister, too, the twin she loved dearly, but felt the need to break away from, to forge her own identity rather than be one of a pair. What she had been oddly reserved about was her parents, which made sense if his mother was right and she was indeed the illegitimate daughter of Sir William. Yet tonight the alcohol had loosened her tongue and she looked eager to spill every last secret.

'There was always something missing. When we were young our mother told Sarah and I that our father was a soldier, killed in some distant war. Even then it felt as though I had been robbed of something and then when I found out he was alive it was as though a part of me was missing. I had this gaping hole that seemed to get bigger and bigger every time I thought about my father, out there somewhere.'

'Sir William?'

Selina looked up at him, realising what she had just given away. She hesitated, as if wondering if she should deny it, but after a moment nodded.

'Yes. Sir William. My father.' Her tone was bitter. 'A man who I suspect would be rather delighted if I quietly wasted away from some horrible disease. I expect he would even pay for a discreet burial, far from the family tomb, of course.'

'He has shown no care for you?'

Selina shook her head, looking down at the ground. He could see the glint of tears in her eyes and finally realised the depth of the turmoil she had been suffering.

'It is my fault for expecting a fairy tale. I've always been fanciful, carried away by my own imagination. My sister, Sarah, tried to tell me that there was nothing to be gained from chasing a man who had not wanted anything to do with us throughout our childhood, but I reasoned things might not be as simple as all that. I spun stories about a man, constrained by the expectations of his family, living in regret, desperate to find the two daughters he had left behind.'

'That wasn't what you found.'

'No. Sir William was aghast when I turned up at his door. His first thought was to turn me away, that was certainly what his wife counselled him to do, but he was worried about his reputation. He is quite the social climber, desperate to be accepted by the higher echelons of Society, hamperedby the mediocrity of his birth.'

'He was worried you would make trouble for him, tell anyone who would listen about the illegitimate daughters he had left behind.'

Selina gave a mirthless snort of laughter. 'It is ridiculous really. The nobility have all these ideals, all these rules they expect everyone to live their lives by, but they get away with flaunting them at every turn.

Show me a viscount or an earl who denies having an illegitimate child or a scandalous mistress and I will show you a liar.'

'I have neither,' Callum said gently.

She paused then and turned to look at him, her eyes meeting his. 'Then you are the exception.'

'I do not know how you have stayed with Sir William for so long.'

'Blind optimism. I think it may be my curse. I kept thinking if I just gave it one more week he would see I wasn't there to ruin his life, that we could have some sort of civil, perhaps even loving relationship.'

'But that never materialised.'

'No. I was almost ready to leave when they announced this trip to Scotland. I thought I would be banished at that point, instructed to disappear, but then there was the suggestion I join them.' She pressed her lips together, trying to not show quite how much all this had hurt her. Callum had the urge to pull her into his arms, to comfort her, but he resisted, thrusting his hands into his pockets to constrain them.

'You thought this might be the softening you had been waiting for.'

'I told myself a few more months could not hurt and perhaps I would regret it if I didn't see if Sir William's attitude towards me would change as he got away from the stresses of London.'

'I am wagering it did not.'

'No, it soon became clear I was still an inconvenience at best and a dirty little secret at worst. He brought me along as he still did not trust me not to reveal to someone who might matter my true connection to him while he was away.'

'I am sorry,' Callum said quietly. 'To have found your father when you thought him lost, only to realise he was never going to acknowledge you or treat you kindly, is horrible.'

'It is my own fault. I am a romantic fool who thinks if I wish for something hard enough it will happen.'

'Do not let this disillusion you, Selina.' He heard the catch in his voice, the thrum of emotion. Selina must have heard it, too, for she turned to him, stopping in the middle of the road and waiting for him to look at her.

This time he did reach out, disobeying every instinct he had that told him to keep walking, to turn the conversation to the mundane and return Selina home with haste. His fingers grazed her cheek and he felt a spark pass between them, hopping from her skin to his and making his fingertips fizz and tingle.

'Do not let this awful man change even a single

little part of you. He does not deserve to mould you in any way.'

Her breathing had quickened, her chest was rising and falling as if she had been walking uphill despite the road being flat. Her lips parted ever so slightly and he saw the very tip of her tongue dart out to moisten them. For a moment he could think of nothing but kissing her, nothing but the taste of her lips, the feel of her skin under his hands. He wanted to forget his obligations, forget the promises he had made, and take what he wanted right here in the wilderness with only the stars and the night creatures as witnesses.

'You're thinking about kissing me,' Selina said, a little smile playing on her lips.

'And you're thinking about being kissed.'

'See,' she said, giving a little shrug of her shoulders. 'I'm doing it again. I know there can be nothing between us. I understand that. Yet here I am wishing you would throw me over the back of your horse and whisk me away into the sunset.'

'What would we do in the sunset?'

'Oh, adorably sickening things. Kiss and cuddle and—' She broke off, blushing, and Callum knew exactly what she was thinking.

'Selina Shepherd, I thought you were meant to be an innocent miss.'

'Is it sinful to wish for something? To imagine, when you know it will never happen?'

Callum felt a yearning deep inside him. Never had he wanted a woman the way he wanted Selina. She was intoxicating, alluring in her honesty and her vulnerability.

'If that is sinful, then call me a sinner,' he murmured, unable to stop himself from taking a step towards her.

'You've...imagined things?'

'Ever since I first met you, you've plagued my dreams. I wake filled with longing, feeling completely unfulfilled, wishing I could dive back into the dream to finish what we started.'

'I dream of you, too.' Her words were barely more than a whisper, but they made something tighten deep inside and he felt a wave of desire flood through him.

'You do?'

She nodded and he thought she wasn't going to say any more, but then she looked away and continued. 'Last night I dreamed of us lying down in the heather together. Somehow, as you do in dreams, we had lost our clothes along the way.'

Callum swallowed hard and felt his eyes flit down to take in Selina's perfect body. He felt as though he already knew every curve, so hungrily had he taken in each time their bodies had brushed together. Yet the idea of stripping her out of her dress and exploring every inch of her by the light of the moon and the stars was almost too much to bear.

'Did you dream of what came next?'

By the colour that flooded to her cheeks Callum could see she had and he felt a need to know what her subconscious had dreamed of. For a long moment she wouldn't meet his eye and then she tilted her chin up and looked at him.

'I did.' It was such a simple statement, but Callum felt all his pent-up desire surge and throb at those two little words and if Selina had not turned away he would have ravished her there on the road between Taigh Blath and Ballachulish. 'Now, I thought you were meant to be seeing me safely home.'

Callum couldn't stop the low groan of frustration that came from his lips and desperately tried to remind himself this was for the best. Right now he could barely remember why he was torturing himself in such a cruel way, especially when Selina clearly wanted the same thing he did.

By the time the silhouette of the house had come into view Callum had managed to regain a little control over himself. He guided Selina away from the main drive, aware that if anyone happened to glance out of one of the windows at the front of the house they would be spotted as clear as if it were day. Instead he led her around the side of the house, using the trees to hide their movement.

'What if the door is locked?' Selina suddenly looked worried. The crisp air had done a wonderful job of sobering her from the last of the alcohol, meaning she was now nervous that they might be caught.

'I expect it will be. We're a friendly lot here in Ballachulish, but I would not leave a house with as many fine things in it as Taigh Blath unlocked all night long. It would be foolish to tempt anyone who might fancy one of the valuable paintings or pieces of porcelain for themselves.'

'How will I get back in?' Selina asked, aghast at the idea that she might be locked out.

'You forget I grew up here. I know every trick to get into this fortress, every window that does not quite close properly, every door that can be gently forced open.'

They were around the back of the house now and Callum paused by a nondescript wooden door, half-hidden by a climbing plant. Selina frowned, taking a step back and looking from side to side.

'What door is this? I haven't noticed it before.'

'It is designed that way,' Callum said, enjoying himself now. 'It looks like many of the other doors dotted around that lead to the service areas of the house, but is tucked out the way to be inconspicuous.'

'Where does it lead?'

'You will have to wait and see.'

He reached out and pulled away a section of the wooden, gripping a hidden latch and quietly opening the door before slipping inside. Selina hesitated behind him, only following him inside when he held out his hand for her.

'When I close the door it will be completely dark,' he warned her. 'Hold my hand and I will guide you along the passage. Use your other hand to feel along the wall.'

She peered uncertainly past him down the passage, although nothing could be seen past the first few feet.

'Will there be rats?'

'Perhaps. It is impossible to completely keep the vermin out in an old house like this. Would you prefer it if I carried you?'

She looked as though she was seriously considering the offer, but eventually shook her head.

'We will be in the dark for about a minute. Be especially careful on the stairs.'

As he reached out to pull the door closed behind him he felt Selina huddle close, her body pressed up against his. Their fingers were entwined and she gripped his hand tight.

'Start walking with me, nice and steady. One foot in front of the other.'

They began to edge along the passageway, Callum counting the steps under his breath. The old house had a number of these passages, built by previous owners in case of attack by the English in a time when hostilities still ran hot between the two nations. Throughout his childhood he had loved discovering the secrets the old house held and as he grew older he would often use them to escape from his father when he was particularly inebriated.

'Careful here, we're going to go up some stairs. They spiral round and are quite narrow, but if you brace yourself against the outer wall you should manage them.'

They started to ascend, climbing up in the complete darkness. Callum counted again, reaching the top after about thirty seconds. From there it was only a few paces to the panel that slid to one side and then they would be in one of the main bedrooms.

Selina let out a sigh of relief as they ducked out of the passageway. Even though it was lighter out here with a lot more space she did not relinquish Callum's hand and from the expression on her face he saw she was still trying to calm her nerves.

Silently he slid the panel back into place, not wanting to risk the passageway being discovered while he saw Selina to her room, then he turned to her.

'Well done, I know many who would not have done that in complete darkness.'

'I kept thinking there must be some light, even just a glimmer, to light the way, but there was nothing. It felt as though I had lost my sight.'

Callum squeezed her hand, wanting to give her time to recove,r but also conscious they could be discovered at any moment by a curious servant or family member if they were unlucky.

'Let us get you back to your room,' he whispered.

'If you want to go…'

'Not before I see you safely to your bedroom.'

She did not argue, still shaken by the climb through the passage, and together they crept out into the hallway. Selina's bedroom was only a few doors away and as they stood on the threshold she turned to face him.

'Thank you for walking me home.'

'It was my pleasure.'

She hesitated and for a moment he wondered if she might lean forward to kiss him. All the desire he had felt earlier on the walk home surged again and he caught hold of her hand, thinking to draw her towards him.

Their eyes met and for an eternity it seemed as

though they were teetering on a precipice and if either took a single step in any direction they would be swept away by an avalanche. Then Selina took a shuddering breath and stepped back, disappearing into her room before he could say anything more. Callum was left staring at the closed door, unable to move for a few seconds, before he remembered where he was. Quickly he retreated, making his way back to the entrance to the passage, filled with longing and regret.

Chapter Thirteen

Selina rose early, feeling tired and unrefreshed. What little sleep she had snatched after the excitement of the dance and the walk home after had been filled with dreams of Callum. Each time she drifted off she was plagued by visions of what might have been, of Callum in various states of undress, ravishing her in a hundred different ways. After each dream she woke hot and breathless and yearning for Callum's touch.

It was a relief when she heard the household stirring, even though she had only managed to snatch a few hours' sleep. Being tired was better than torturing herself with dreams of a man who was soon to be married to her half-sister.

Selina dressed slowly, taking her time to brush out her hair, pulling at the tangles from the night before. When she was finally ready she surveyed herself in the little mirror on the wall and deemed the reflection presentable. There were dark rings under her eyes, but she doubted the Kingsleys would look at her long enough to notice.

As she left her room and started towards the stairs she was surprised to find Catherine marching up to meet her, a grim look on her face.

'Good morning,' Selina greeted her, trying to sound cheery.

'Hardly.' Catherine caught Selina by the arm and forcibly propelled her back into the little bedroom, closing the door firmly behind her.

'Is something amiss?' Selina asked as Catherine stood by the door, glaring at her.

'Harlot.'

'Excuse me.'

'Don't try to play the innocent little miss. I see through your deception.'

'Catherine, I have no idea what you are talking about.' Selina tried to remain calm, but a shiver of fear ran through her. Catherine was normally spiteful rather than outright cruel, but today she had a wild look about her as if she might be capable of anything.

'Last night. I saw you sneaking in with Lord Leven, leading him to your bedroom.'

Selina felt the blood drain from her face and suddenly she felt light headed. Reaching behind her, she felt her bed and sank down on to it.

'It isn't what you think.'

Catherine snorted with derision. 'I suppose you invited him back to play a game of chess or discuss something as mundane as ornithology.'

'Nothing happened. Lord Leven was merely ensuring I got home safely.'

'You were meant to be home already. I saw you leave the dance, you told everyone you were coming back to Loch View Lodge, but instead it was just a ruse wasn't it? To give you time to seduce *my* future husband.'

'No.' Selina shook her head desperately. It was difficult to justify, difficult to defend herself. She had been in the wrong. Instead of coming home as she had said she would, she'd attended the party for the locals in the barn. She'd welcomed Callum's offer to walk her home, even though she knew spending time with him alone was dangerous. And she had stood in the doorway to this very room wishing he would kiss her, wishing he would take her in his arms and ravish her on the narrow bed.

'Nothing happened,' Selina repeated.

Catherine took another step forward. 'So you were here all night, were you? Tucked up in bed?'

'No. I admit I went to a party, after the dance Sir William arranged. It was for the locals, held in one of the big barns close by.'

'You went unchaperoned.'

'Lord Leven's mother was there and plenty of the other village women.'

'If you were a lady, this would be enough to ruin you,' Catherine spat. 'But bastard children have no reputation to lose anyway. Perhaps you should be thankful for that.'

Trying to ignore Catherine's barbed words Selina pressed on. 'In the early hours of the morning Lord Leven offered to escort me home. He knew a way into the house that meant we wouldn't need to wake the servants. He saw me upstairs, to the hallway outside my bedroom, and then he left, Catherine.'

'You think that just because you did not manage to seduce him while the rest of the household slept it makes everything else you did acceptable.'

'No,' Selina said quietly. 'I know it is not. I shouldn't have gone to the party in the barn and I shouldn't have agreed to Lord Leven walking me home.'

'He is *my* fiancé, near enough. In a few weeks I will marry him and you will return to your penniless life of drudgery. Why do you insist on trying to jeopardise things for me?' There was a hint of petulance in Catherine's tone, but Selina saw the anguish there as well.

'You keep throwing yourself at Lord Leven. How

do you not understand—he is going to marry me. *You* are not made for marriage with a man like that. Perhaps he thinks to amuse himself with a dalliance for a few days, but you are worthless, Selina Shepherd. No decent man is going to want to marry you.'

'I'm sorry,' Selina said quietly. 'I know things have not been easy for you since we arrived in Ballachulish.'

'Things would be easier if you would just go away. Crawl back to whatever dingy hovel you came from.'

'I will be gone soon,' Selina said softly. 'I will be far away in England and you will be here, married to Lord Leven.'

'Don't you forget it,' Catherine said, her voice low and dangerous. 'I have been waiting to marry for years, always on the peripheries while my father advises patience so I can be the head of a worthy household. Now is my time. I will be Countess of Leven. I will be Lord Leven's wife and my son will be the next Earl of Leven.'

Selina saw the raw ambition in Catherine's eyes and felt a chill of fear. She had always assumed it was Sir William driving this match, but she realised Catherine was just as keen. She wanted the title and the old family name, she wanted all her old friends to have to call her Lady Leven, to acknowledge her superiority in rank.

For too long Selina had viewed Catherine as a spoiled, spiteful girl. They had done nothing but argue since Selina had arrived at Sir William's house to inform the man she was his illegitimate daughter. Now she was fast realising that Catherine was indeed spoiled and certainly often spiteful, but there was more to her than that. She was ruthless and ambitious and would think nothing of destroying Selina to get what she wanted.

Selina reminded herself that soon she would finally be free of the Kingsleys, even if that meant also leaving Callum behind. The rational part of her had accepted they could not be together. His mission was to buy back the land his father had lost, to secure the future of the people of Ballachulish. That meant he *had* to marry Catherine. Selina might feel a little heartbroken, but she had seen there was no other way. Yet the idea of leaving Callum behind, of returning to England knowing she would never see him again in her life, made her heart ache in her chest.

'Stay away from Lord Leven or I will ensure the whole world knows what a whore you really are and I will persuade Papa to drive you away with no money and none of the clothes he's paid for this past year.'

Selina watched as her half-sister flounced out. Once she was sure Catherine was gone she slumped onto the bed and blew out a loud breath. Her hands were shaking. She had no doubt if her father found out she had been sneaking around with Lord Leven he would deal with her harshly. She did not want much from the man, but with no funds of her own she needed him to arrange her transport for the journey back to England.

After a few minutes her pulse had slowed and her hands stopped shaking, but Selina was still not ready to face the rest of the Kingsleys. Catherine had not told of Callum's late-night visit to the house yet, but at the slightest provocation she might decide to tell their father. Then everything would be over for Selina.

Chapter Fourteen

Callum hefted the axe up in his right hand, feeling the weight of it, and turned to the painted target on the tall tree in front of him. He breathed deeply, blocking out the noise from the world around him, allowing nothing to exist but him and the weapon in his hand. He hefted it back over his shoulder, adjusted his position slightly and then threw, watching critically as it spun through the air and then landed with a satisfying thud, embedded in the trunk of the tree.

'Am I to gather you've had a bad day?' Bruce asked him from his position a few feet away.

'What makes you think that?'

'You always throw best when you're in a bad mood.'

'That's ridiculous.'

His friend shrugged, holding up his fingers to count off as he spoke next. 'That time the Williams brothers were thrown into prison for trespassing.

When Joanna Rigby refused to walk out with you. When your father gave you a black eye when he thought you were an intruder trying to steal all of Taigh Blath's treasures.'

'They are the instances you think I've thrown best?'

'Aye. There's no arguing. Ever since we were lads you've always needed a crisis to sharpen your mind.'

Callum walked over to the tree trunk and pulled at the axe. It was wedged firmly into the wood and he needed to brace his foot against the exposed roots of the tree to get a good purchase. Once free he took it to Bruce and handed it over.

The large man squared his shoulders and took up a stance with feet wide apart and knees slightly bent. Callum remained quiet while Bruce prepared his shot, watching the axe sail through the air, thrown with ease by the big man and landing a little off centre in the trunk.

'Maybe I need to find myself a girl to pine over. Might make my throws more accurate.'

'Or perhaps just leave off the whisky before breakfast.'

Bruce took his time removing the axe from the tree, walking back to Callum with an unhurried gait.

'You're itching to snatch this axe off me. It won't save you from your heartache.'

'This has nothing to do with Miss Shepherd,' Callum said, grabbing the axe from Bruce's hand. 'I am just a man who wants to throw an axe into a tree. There need not be anything more to it than that.'

'If you say so.'

'I do.'

'Good.' Bruce was silent for a few seconds and then sighed and spoke again. 'Look, everyone is tiptoeing around you, but I think you need some good, old-fashioned, straight talking.'

'From you?' Callum threw the axe, irritated when it curved to the side and struck the tree at an angle.

'Who better? I've known you for twenty-five years and I am one of the few people around here who does not have a vested interest in what decisions you make about your future.'

Bruce was a landowner in his own right. Although his family were not titled, many generations earlier they had acquired some land. Through cautious investments and careful management what they owned grew. A few years ago Bruce had inherited a thriving estate and a few properties on the land adjacent to that now owned by Sir William. It was not huge, about a tenth of the size of the estate Callum's father had lost, but it was securely his. He did not need Callum to guarantee his future in Ballachulish, as so many other people did.

Callum retrieved the axe and passed it to Bruce.

'Endow me with your wisdom then.'

'Not here. Too many things with a sharp edge around. Let us go and get a drink and set the world to rights.'

The local inn was only a short walk away and before long they were settled on a table in the corner of the dark room. Despite the sunshine outside, the main room of the Lost Sheep Inn was dingy and filled with smoke from a fire that wasn't really needed. There were some tables set on a patch of grass out the front of the inn, rickety things fixed together with rusty nails and splintering wood, but these were all full on such a fine day and Callum didn't want anyone to overhear whatever difficult truths Bruce was going to confront him with.

'You're torturing yourself unnecessarily,' Bruce said eventually once they had their drinks in front of them.

'Hardly. Do you think I am enjoying this?'

'I have to wonder.'

Callum sighed. 'I know what needs to be done. It is all I have been working towards for over a decade. It is why I spent so long in the frozen wastelands of Canada before coming home.'

'No one is denying your noble sacrifice,' Bruce murmured.

'You're mocking me.'

'You were eighteen when your father died. Eighteen when the creditors swooped in and took everything. You were not to blame.'

'I know. I do not blame myself.'

'I think you do, somewhere deep down.'

'I feel a sense of responsibility for the people who should have had a secure future living and working on the Thomson estate, but I do not think I am the one who lost it.'

'You shoulder your father's sins…'

'Is there a point to this, Bruce?' Callum said a little sharper than he meant to. The last few days had been difficult and he did not wish to get into a debate as to who was to blame for ruining the lives of all the locals.

'You have this notion that you must restore what was lost. That it is your responsibility to give people back their homes and security.'

'I am Earl of Leven; it *is* my responsibility.'

'At what cost?'

Callum was silent. He thought of Catherine Kingsley. The woman who was going to one day very soon be his wife. Then he thought of Selina Shepherd and the undeniable attraction he felt for her, the connection they shared.

'By marrying Miss Kingsley you will regain control over some of the land you lost and likely have influence over anything Sir William does not give as his daughter's dowry. Yet you will be miserable, married to a woman you do not care about, stuck with her for the next forty years knowing you let the one you loved slip through your fingers.'

'I know, Bruce,' Callum said quietly. He wondered if his friend was right. Maybe he did love Selina. He certainly felt something he had never felt before. 'But what can I do? If I marry Miss Shepherd, Sir William will keep control of the land and probably start clearing it of tenants out of sheer spite.'

'So you have considered it?' Bruce said quietly.

Callum nodded. He had thought little else of what his life would be like if he married Selina recently. He could not get her from his mind.

'I do not profess to have the answer, but I feel as though you are making a terrible mistake,' Bruce said as he took a long gulp of beer. 'What sort of friend would I be if I let you go ahead with something that I knew would make you unhappy?' He looked at Callum squarely. 'You cannot have everything, but it is still your choice what you do decide to have. Happiness is within your reach and no one here in Ballachulish would resent you for choosing the path that led to your contentment.'

Callum shook his head. 'But they would. Not outwardly. The people here are good people, kind people, but the resentment would start to build. They would wonder what gives me the right to choose my own happiness over their survival.'

Bruce remained silent and Callum sighed. 'I wish there was a way. I wish more than anything there was some way that I could be with Miss Shepherd and not condemn the locals to land clearances and evictions.'

He drained his mug of beer and clapped his old friend on the shoulder, standing up and surveying the room before making for the door. There wasn't an easy solution to his problem and he needed to stop delaying the inevitable. This afternoon he would go to Taigh Blath and insist he and Sir William finalised the contract that would see him marry Catherine Kingsley and regain control of the land around Ballachulish.

'You look very determined my love,' Lady Leven said, hurrying to catch her son as he strode down the main street of the village.

'I am on my way to see Sir William. I want to get this whole affair finished and finalised.'

'Except it won't be finished, will it?'

Callum turned to his mother, frowning. 'What do you mean? He can hardly go back on his word once it is put to paper in a legal document.'

'I wasn't talking of Sir William. I was talking about Miss Kingsley.' Lady Leven slipped her arm through Callum's and gently guided him off the main path. There was a footpath that led through the trees to a quiet area where she liked to walk and it was here she led Callum now. 'You will be married to Miss Kingsley. That is something that will last a lifetime.'

'Are you and Bruce conspiring together?'

'Mr Bruce is a good man. Am I to gather he's had words with you, too?'

'I have just come from the Lost Sheep where he imparted his worries over a mug of beer.'

'Listen to him. He's wise and successful.'

Callum fell silent for a while, wondering why his closest friends and family seemed intent on cautioning him today.

'Have I ever told you of your father's courtship of me?' Lady Leven said, gazing out at the beautiful view in front of them.

'No.'

'I didn't think so,' she sighed. 'It was non-existent. I met him three times before we married and two of those times he barely said more than a word of greeting.'

'It was arranged by your father?' It was hardly the surprise. Although a drunk in private, the late Lord Leven would have been viewed as quite the catch. His mother was English, from a family of impoverished aristocrats who no doubt thought they were sending their daughter to a better life north of the border. Either that or they were just glad of one less mouth to feed.

'Yes. I was devastated. I was in love, you see, but not with your father. Mr Pennington...' She stared out into the distance for a moment, lost in her memories. 'He was the second son of a baron. His elder brother was due to inherit so he had carved out a nice little career for himself in the clergy. I think I would have liked the life of a vicar's wife.'

'Your father would not entertain it?'

His mother sighed and looked at him. 'I did not fight for what I wanted. I accepted my family's pleas to try to restore our fortunes by marrying Lord Leven, thinking my sacrifice would be noble.' She inhaled sharply. 'It was not noble. Your father was a drunkard even in the early days of our marriage and as the years went on I became more discontent with my life. You were the only shining light in that gloomy existence.'

'I knew it could not have been a happy marriage,'

Callum said quietly. 'Who could be happy married to *him*?'

'Perhaps someone could. Someone who had not known what it was like to feel her heart sing when she looked at the face of the man she loved, when she felt his hand graze across hers. I did what was expected of me, I did my duty and all it brought me was unhappiness.' She took his hand in her own. 'I do not want the same for you. I have seen how you look at Miss Shepherd, it is clear for the whole world to see. She is unattached and would make a lovely Lady Leven, even if you did not have Taigh Blath to live in and the estate to rule over.'

Callum did not answer for a long while, looking out ahead of him and considering his mother's words. She had always allowed him to make his own decisions, even when they impacted her. She had supported him when he had declared he was using what little funds he had to board the ship to Canada despite it meaning she was left all alone in the tiny little cottage in the village where she had once been the highest pinnacle of society.

'I will not tell you what to do, my love, but I ask you to really consider what it is you want. Perhaps this once you could think of yourself and your own desires and not what everyone else expects of you.'

'How can I hold my head up high in Ballachulish

if I send Sir William away and with it any chance to regain the land my father lost? People will be turned out of their properties, thrown off the land.'

'Then perhaps you admit you cannot do this alone, that you cannot single-handedly restore what was lost. It may be you have to think of another way to help these people, a way that does not involve you sacrificing your happiness for theirs.' She reached out and cupped his cheek, affection in her eyes. 'You have always been a proud man, Callum, always thought you need to do everything yourself. It is something I have always loved about you, but do not let it be the thing that is your downfall.'

Callum felt the words pierce through his heart. He *was* proud. He wanted to be the person who achieved things and he never liked asking for help. Much of the time he dressed it up in his mind as a positive part of his character, but he knew sometimes it could be negative.

'I will leave you to think about it,' Lady Leven said, squeezing his hand. 'I hope by tomorrow I might have a lovely new daughter-in-law-to-be.'

She disappeared quietly, moving off down the path with poise and grace. Even throughout the difficult years she had never let go of the way she was raised. She was first and foremost a lady, whatever else she might be now.

Callum walked a little further and then sank down to the ground, propping his back against the trunk of a large tree. He could not ignore both his mother and Bruce's words, especially when they said the same thing, but he found it hard to see how he could take a path other than the one he was hurtling down.

He allowed himself to dream, to imagine Selina as his wife, walking through the glens and around the lochs hand in hand with a woman he loved. It was a captivating fantasy, but he could not see how it could be his reality, not without letting a lot of people down.

After fifteen minutes of contemplation he was no closer to an answer. He walked back towards the village, meaning to go home and think some more when he was accosted by Bruce. The big bear of a man must have been looking out for him for he pounced as soon as he saw Callum.

'Forgive me for earlier,' he said, pulling Callum into an embrace. 'It is not my place to tell you what to do. Come, let us drink and talk of other things, of our escapades of years gone by, and forget your dilemma of the day.'

'I don't think…' Callum began to say, but Bruce was already pulling him towards the tavern they had left not an hour earlier.

'Come, a couple of drinks will do you no harm.'

Callum had a sneaking suspicion that Bruce was worried that he would march up to Taigh Blath and demand to see Sir William to settle things once and for all. His friend wanted to do anything to give Callum a little time to consider his actions. Today, Callum did not mind this manipulation—in fact, he relished the idea of forgetting about his responsibilities for a few hours.

Chapter Fifteen

Selina blew out the candle beside her bed and wriggled down under the bedsheets. It might have been a warm day for the Scottish Highlands, but the nights still had a chill about them and she was grateful for the extra blanket she had purloined from one of the unoccupied rooms.

She had kept to her bedroom for most of the afternoon, making her way through a couple of the books she had taken from the extensive library at Taigh Blath. She hadn't wanted to see anyone and up here she had been left alone. At dinnertime she had sent her apologies, saying she had a headache. Thankfully one of the maids had taken pity on her and sent a tray with some bread and cheese and leftover cake to her room, otherwise her grumbling belly might have forced her downstairs.

Selina closed her eyes, hoping sleep would come and take her. She wanted a dreamless night, to be able to revel in the oblivion of a restful sleep and wake rejuvenated and fresh in the morning.

Almost immediately the image of Callum slipped into her mind. She thought of how he'd looked at her when they'd walked home from the dance. He'd gazed at her with such an air of longing she had felt her resolve waver and the attraction once again flare.

Banishing the memory from her mind, she tried to think of anything else. Flowers and bumblebees and the way the sea sucked at the sand as the tide went out at the beach. It worked for a minute, but then Callum sneaked into her picture, wet from the spray of the sea, his shirt sticking to his muscular body.

'Stop it,' she told herself crossly. 'Sleep.'

She turned over, squeezing her eyes tightly shut now to try to trick her brain into complying.

As she turned there was a clink on the glass of the window. She stiffened, but then reasoned it was probably just the wind making everything in the old house shift. She had just convinced herself to relax when there was a second clink and then a third.

Wishing she had not blown out her candle, she rose from bed and stepped across the small room to the window. The view outside was shielded by heavy red curtains, made of a thick velvet that once must have cost a fortune, but now the edges were fraying and the material faded.

Unsure why she felt so nervous and reminding herself she did not believe in ghosts, she gripped the edges of the curtains and then pulled them back.

At first nothing was visible in the darkness, but as she looked down at the garden stretching out ahead of her the moon came out from behind a cloud and she saw Callum standing below, his arm drawn back ready to throw another stone at her window.

Selina felt a thrill of excitement that she quickly quashed. If she had any sense she would send him away without even talking to him. Even him merely being outside Taigh Blath was inviting questions she did not want to answer.

She felt for the fastenings that held the window closed and tugged at them. They were stiff from years of misuse and creaked terribly when she finally managed to draw them back. The window only opened a crack, but it was enough for her to show Callum he had her attention.

'Selina, I need to talk to you,' he called up, his voice carrying much further than was wise on the quiet night.

'Go home, Callum. We can talk in the morning.'

'I need to see you now.'

Selina frowned, wondering if he was drunk. He had told her of his father and his dependence on alcohol, and had always remained in control, even at the local dance where there were plenty of people in their cups. Yet tonight his words were not as clear, not as sharp, and she wasn't sure if he was swaying a little.

'Come down and open the door,' he half-whispered, but his voice was loud enough to carry all the way up to the window.

'Go home, Callum,' Selina repeated, wondering if he would go away if she closed the window and pulled the curtain or if he would find a more disruptive way to get into the house. He'd spoken of multiple hidden passageways and secret openings concealed in Taigh Blath. She couldn't risk him taking one that might take him past Sir William or Lady Kingsley's room.

'Please, Selina.' He clasped his hands together in front of him and looked so earnest she felt her resolve waver. He must have sensed the change in her demeanour for he took a step forward and then another.

'Wait there,' she instructed. 'And do not make a sound.'

Knowing she was going to regret her actions, Selina shut the window and silently padded across the room to the door. She opened it a crack, listening intently before stepping out on to the landing.

Selina paused, wondering whether to go down the main stairs and let Callum in through the front door or whether to try the passage he had shown her the other day. The thought of trying to navigate the passage in the darkness by herself made her shudder and Selina quickly decided on risking the main stairs.

She took her time, trying to remember where there were creaky floorboards and where was safe to stop, but four times she had to stop, her muscles tense with anticipation and terror, convinced the loud creaks must have woken someone up.

Finally she was downstairs and as swiftly as possible she retrieved the key for the front door from its spot on a hook in the passage to the kitchen. As quietly as she could she unlocked the massive front door and poked her head out.

Callum was there in an instant, darting inside the house. Before she could open her mouth to admonish him for his reckless behaviour he stepped close, placing a finger on her lips.

'Hush, I know I should not be here, lass. I just needed to see you, that was all.' He grinned at her and gave her a cheeky wink. 'You're glad to see me, though.'

'If anyone sees you here...'

'They better not see me, then.'

He took her by the hand and pulled her with him, pointing out what spots to avoid as they ascended the stairs. With Callum's knowledge of the house they were much quieter and much quicker going upstairs and within two minutes they were in Selina's bedroom with the door firmly closed and locked behind them.

'Now I am glad the rest of the family are in a completely different part of the house,' Selina murmured.

'As am I.'

They were standing a few feet apart and Selina suddenly felt self-conscious. She was in her nightgown, a demure garment made of thick white cotton that reached from the base of her throat all the way down to her ankles. It was hardly an outfit that invited immoral thoughts, but Callum was regarding her as if he were a fox ready to pounce on an unsuspecting rabbit.

'You've been drinking,' Selina said, trying to work out his motivation for coming here this evening.

'I have, although I am not so drunk you have to worry I will not remember this in the morning.'

'Would you have come here if you were sober?'

He seemed to take a moment to consider the question and then blew out his cheeks. 'Truly, Selina, I do not know. I have had the strangest day and I cannot think what I would have done if even one part of it were different.'

Selina took a step closer, unable to stop herself.

'Why are you here, Callum?'

'As I was sitting in the tavern, drinking terrible

beer with my oldest friend, I realised I needed to talk to you. My head was in a jumble and I knew I would not sleep until I had seen you.'

'It must be important for you to come here at night.'

'Yes. It is.'

He held out his hand and as if in a dream Selina stepped forward and took it. She thought he might kiss her, but instead he led her to the narrow bed and sat down, making space for her to sit down beside him.

It was dark in the room, although Selina had left the curtains open a sliver and a beam of moonlight shone through the gap. Most of Callum's face was in darkness, but she could see his eyes, shining as he looked at her.

'All day long I have been pulled this way and that. For so long my focus has been on doing the right thing by the people of Ballachulish, my people, that I have denied all personal desires. Yet with you I cannot ignore what I feel.'

'What is it you feel?'

'I do not want you to leave Scotland. I do not wish to never see you again.'

'You know that cannot be. I need to move forward with my life.'

'I know,' he said and Selina felt herself deflate a little. Part of her had wondered if this was the declaration she had been hoping for, his promise that he would fight for her, that he would choose her over anything and everything else. That was what she wanted deep down, whatever brave front she presented outwardly. 'I know that, but still I cannot rid myself of thoughts of you. You plague my waking hours and my sleep. I am captivated by you.'

He shifted a little, his hand coming to rest on her leg, and she felt the skin under her nightgown pucker into goose pimples. Never had she imagined being so physically attracted to another person that a mere hint of a touch would affect her so much. 'It sounds terrible, but I want to possess you. I want to make you mine and never share you with anyone else. I want to lock you away from the world in my bedroom so there are no distractions, no interruptions.'

Selina's heart was pounding in her chest and she knew she would willingly do anything Callum suggested. Her virtue was one of her most valuable things, but one look from Callum and she would throw it away in an instant.

'The desire I feel for you is almost uncontrollable,' Callum said, his voice low and anguished, 'but I feel so much more. I think I was trying to pretend what I felt for you was just physical, that it was an attraction that would pass as soon as you were out of sight, but

I was lying, Selina. What I feel for you is so much more than a physical desire.'

'What do you mean?' Her voice was barely more than a whisper. This was not how she had envisioned her night unfolding and she thought Callum was about to make a declaration that would have far-reaching consequences.

He took his time, lacing his fingers through hers and adjusting the curtain so he could see her clearly.

'I love you, Selina Shepherd. I think I started to fall in love with you that first night by the loch and every moment we have spent together since has deepened that love.'

'You love me?'

'Yes. I do. I love you *and* I desire you.'

Inside her chest Selina's heart swelled. Never had she thought Callum would declare his love for her. The whole situation had been a mess from the very first time they had met, complicated by Callum's sense of duty to the locals and Selina's unsympathetic family. Yet all that seemed inconsequential if Callum loved her.

'I honestly do not know what the future holds, Selina. I cannot see how to make things work so everyone is happy, but I was sitting in the tavern and I realised that I loved you and I knew I could not keep that to myself.'

'You love me?' Selina asked again, still not able to quite believe it. She felt the thrill of his words before a coldness settled upon her. 'You love me, but you cannot be with me.'

Callum looked away, the pain evident on his face. 'I am sorry,' he said, his voice low and desperate. 'I should not have said anything. I know this makes everything worse, yet I could not keep it to myself.'

Selina knew she should feel angry towards him, yet all she could summon was sorrow. Callum was a good man, a noble man. He had set his mind to righting the wrongs his father had committed, to helping the friends and family who had suffered when the land was sold off to Sir William. For years he had worked towards this goal and now, with the end finally in sight, his heart was tearing him in two.

'I love you, too, Callum,' she said quietly. It was all she had to give him and she knew it did not change anything, but she had to say it all the same.

'You love me?'

She nodded. 'Even though I know we are doomed, I know we cannot end up together, I still love you.'

Their eyes met, desire and longing and love pulsing between them until Selina stood up, stepping away to put some distance between them.

'You need to go, Callum, before we do something we regret.'

'Would we regret it?'

'Yes,' she said firmly. 'It would change nothing. You would still have to go ahead with the marriage to Catherine.'

He groaned but nodded. 'You are right, of course. I apologise for coming here tonight. I just needed to see you. Bruce and my mother were going on about following my heart, yet I cannot reconcile myself with the idea of letting everyone down.'

'I know, my love. That is why you must leave before anyone finds you here.'

He stood, taking a few steps towards her before taking her hands in his own.

'One kiss,' he said, 'Can we at least share one more kiss?'

Unable to refuse her own desire, she swayed closer, feeling the tears pricking at her eyes and dropping on to her cheeks as they kissed.

Before she was ready he was gone, slipping from the room and away through the house as if he were an apparition.

Chapter Sixteen

It was a beautiful morning, the sky blue and the sun glinting off the waters of the loch. Selina had managed to escape the oppressive atmosphere of Taigh Blath, slipping out while Sir William was busy with his business correspondence and Lady Kingsley and Catherine were out calling on Lady Leven.

Selina felt numb this morning, shocked by the revelation the night before when Callum had sat beside her on her little single bed and declared that he loved her. For a moment she had allowed herself to dream, to imagine a life with the man she loved, but then reality had taken over. His declaration changed nothing, not really. He was still engaged to be married to Catherine, still determined to do whatever it took to restore his family's lands. So here she was heartbroken, pining for a man who had never really been hers.

She let out a shuddering breath and tried to focus on the landscape around her. Although the countryside was vast, with the greens of the hills and mountains interspersed with the blue of the lochs as far as the eye could see, Selina had become familiar with this little patch of the Highlands the last few weeks. Her solitary walks took her on different routes down to the loch and she now did not think she would get lost as long as she stuck to one of the familiar paths.

Now she was skirting the edge of the loch, gazing at the glimmering water and wondering if it would be foolish to shed her stockings and her boots and dip a toe into the water. Close by there was a sloping bank that led to a narrow strip of muddy sand, one of the few points where the loch was accessible. She longed to feel the cool water against her skin, thinking of all the times she had paddled in the cold waters off the beach in Hastings.

Here the surface of the loch was calm, almost as smooth as the glass in a mirror. She could not imagine it was a dangerous place to paddle, even though Callum had called the loch treacherous that first night they had met. It had been different then, the water murky and rough, the wind whipping it in all directions.

A paddle cannot hurt, she told herself.

If the water was deeper than it looked, or filled with weeds that tangled her legs, she would retreat to the safety of the little beach.

Before she started stripping off her boots and stockings she checked in all directions, ensuring there was no one watching her. The whole area was deserted. Often on her walks Selina didn't see another person for hours on end. She doubted anyone would be walking past today of all days.

Carefully she perched on a fallen branch of a tree, pulling off her boots and stockings before sinking her toes into the sand. With one last check behind her she lifted up the hem of her dress, gathered the layers of petticoats and then stepped into the water.

It was blissful. The water of the loch was bitingly cold and after half a minute Selina felt as though she could not feel her toes. Despite this the water was so refreshing, so inviting that she took a step deeper and then another. Her feet sunk down into the thick mud at the bottom, anchoring her in place.

Selina exhaled deeply, feeling some of the stress of the last few weeks begin to melt away. The sun was warm and she turned her face up towards it, not caring if she developed a smattering of freckles on her nose. Moments like this reminded her what was truly important in the world and made her realise what a small part of it she really was. It was grounding.

Out here in the loch she could forget her broken heart and the sorrow she felt for what would never be between her and Callum, out here in the loch all she needed to think about was the icy water lapping at her shins and the sunshine on her upturned face.

For a few minutes Selina stayed where she was, her feet sinking a little deeper into the mud at the bottom of the loch. She liked the cool sensation between her toes and lifted her dress a little higher to avoid any splashes of water on her hem. She doubted the Kingsleys would notice if she returned with a slightly damp dress, but it wasn't worth risking their curiosity or their ire.

She had closed her eyes to best enjoy the moment when she heard a splash behind. Her heart skipped in her chest as she twisted her body to see what had caused the noise. To her surprise Hamish was racing towards her in the water, tongue hanging out, looking thrilled to have found her. As yet Callum was nowhere to be seen, but Selina did not doubt he would be far behind. She felt torn, instinctively excited to see him, but reluctant for an encounter that would make the ache in her heart any worse.

Hamish barked, jumping up and splashing her with water, his tail wagging in a show of excitement. Selina laughed, unable to feel anything but affection for the friendly little dog. She transferred the bundle of her skirt and petticoat to one hand and reach down to scratch behind his ears.

'Hamish, leave poor Miss Shepherd alone,' Callum's voice called out from behind them.

Selina tried to turn to face the shore, feeling the pull of the mud on her feet as she attempted to lift them. She was off balance, her feet completely stuck in the mud, and the twisting movement set her wobbling. For a moment Selina thought she would be able to right herself as she felt one foot come loose from the sucking mud, but the other was still trapped and she felt her body topple as she lost her balance completely.

She opened her mouth to scream, but as her body hit the icy cold water the breath was knocked out of her lungs and no sound came out. Although she had been in the shallows she was almost completely submerged, such was the angle of her fall and even her head plunged under the water.

She came up gasping just as strong arms looped under her shoulders and pulled her up out of the water. Callum didn't seem to be bothered by the cold and he held her body to his as he turned and strode back to the bank. Only once they were on dry land did he set her down.

She looked up, meaning to thank him, but stopped when she saw his expression.

'You're laughing at me.'

'You have to admit it was comical. The way you

fell over so slowly. Why didn't you even put your hands out to save yourself?'

'I could have drowned.'

'In eight inches of water? Now that would be impressive.' She shivered and suddenly Callum was serious. 'What could kill you is a chill. Your body is probably still weak from the last time you got soaked and stayed out too long.'

'I can't go back to Taigh Blath like this.'

'I'm sure no one will take any notice.'

Normally Selina would agree, but surely someone would notice her traipsing in half of the water from Loch Leven on her dress.

'I can't. I'll wait until I dry out.'

'Don't be foolish. That dress of yours will take hours to dry, let alone whatever it is you wear underneath.' He eyed her for a moment as if imagining the chemise and petticoats plastered to her body.

'It will dry in the sunshine. It is the warmest day we've had since I arrived here.'

'The weather is hardly tropical. You'll be lucky if your dress is dry in three days.'

Selina grimaced wondering if she would be able to sneak into Taigh Blath without being seen and dismissing the idea. If Lady Kingsley caught her she would take great pleasure in reprimanding her for ruining another dress and use it as evidence that

Selina was reckless with her possessions and did not value what Sir William had given her.

'We could dry it at your house,' Selina suggested, a note of desperation in her voice.

'I live in a little cottage on the other side of the village. We would have to walk the length of the main street to get to it. The gossip would reach Sir William's ears before you returned home.'

Selina bit her lip, looking down at the soggy dress. She was starting to feel uncomfortable, her petticoat was clinging to her legs and despite the sunshine she was beginning to shiver.

After a few moments of silence Callum took pity on her. 'Come on, lass, I'll get a fire started and you can dry off by that. Once you're not dripping wet you'll have to risk sneaking back into Taigh Blath.'

Feeling a flood of relief, Selina looked at Callum's outstretched hand. To take it would be to concede to an intimacy that she wanted so badly, but that she knew could not be. He saw her hesitate and adjusted his position, offering her his arm instead.

Together they walked a little distance around the edge of the loch on a grassy path. Hamish trotted ahead, sniffing every bush and wagging his tail at each new scent he picked up. He was already nearly dry from his dip in the loch.

Neither Selina nor Callum spoke of the night before, of their declarations of love or the sadness they had felt as they parted, but it hung there, heavy, between them, stopping the normal flow of conversation and building in Selina's mind until she could think of nothing else.

'This way,' Callum said, turning away from the water and weaving through the trees until he came to a little clearing. 'Find some dry wood for the fire. The more we have the sooner you'll warm up and dry off a bit.'

Despite the uncomfortable sensation of the wet clothes clinging to her skin Selina moved quickly, eager to get a roaring fire started. She gathered armfuls of sticks bringing them back to the centre clearing where Callum arranged them in a neat little pyramid shape.

'Do you have a tinderbox?'

'No,' he said, not looking up at her, intent on his task. Selina felt her eyes widen as Callum pulled out a knife and then cast around on the ground for the right sort of stone. He had laid some dry grass on the top of the pile of sticks and now he was flicking the knife against the stone, patiently repeating the action over and over until there was a big enough spark to light the grass. As soon as the grass caught alight he bent low, sheltering the fledgling flame from the wind and then as it took hold blowing on the fire gently. Only once he was satisfied that the sticks were starting to burn did he rise up.

'Another skill you picked up in your time in Canada?'

'If you couldn't make a fire you were a dead man,' he said with a shrug. 'I learned fast.'

Selina crouched down in front of it, feeling the first glow of warmth from the small fire.

'You need to take that dress off.'

'Undress? Out here in the forest where anyone could see.'

'I doubt there is anyone but us for miles.'

'If someone came across us with me in a state of undress, no matter how innocent it really was, they would assume the worst.'

'True.' Callum nodded and then whistled for Hamish who had been exploring the woodland nearby. 'Stand guard,' he ordered.

The little dog immediately stiffened as if standing to attention and then moved a distance away, ears pricked and head raised.

'Hamish was bred as a hunting dog, but he is an exceptional guard dog. He will bark before anyone can get within fifty feet of us. Enough warning for you to quickly dress again.' He shrugged. 'It is your choice, but that material is thick and I doubt it will dry with you still in it.'

'Will you help with the fastenings?'

Callum didn't move for a minute and then stepped forward, motioning for her to turn around. His fingers were gentle at her back, unlacing gently until the material of her dress loosened. A couple of times his fingers trailed against the skin of her neck, sending a shiver of anticipation through her body, but Selina did her very best to ignore it.

It would be so easy to turn around, to take a step closer to Callum and raise her lips to his. There was something magical, other-worldly, about this spot in the woods, as if they were shielded from reality, but Selina knew that was just an illusion. Anything they did here would have far-reaching consequences.

She glanced back over her shoulder and her eyes met his, lingering for a long moment. There was longing in his eyes that matched her own and he raised a hand to trail across the sensitive skin at the nape of her neck, but just as soon as she felt his touch it was gone and Callum had stepped away, clearing his throat.

'I will give you some privacy,' he said, his voice gruff.

Carefully Selina slipped her dress off, shivering as the air hit her exposed skin. She was far from naked, with her chemise and stays and petticoat, but they were all white cotton and had become soaked in the loch, giving them a translucent quality.

'Take my jacket,' Callum said, holding it out to her, still studiously looking in the other direction.

Selina took it, grateful for the warmth it provided as she slipped her arms into the sleeves, and then crouched down by the fire.

It did not take long for her to start warming up. The day was not cold and the fire was blazing now, consuming the wood they had piled high.

Callum approached, rolling over a mossy log for her to sit on, positioning it so it was close to the fire but not so close she risked setting her petticoats alight. She thought he might sit next to her, but before he joined her he gathered together a few sturdy fallen branches, leaning them together to make a triangular structure and then draped her dress carefully across it, close to the fire.

Only then did he sit down, right at the other end of the mossy log.

'Thank you,' Selina said quietly. 'I will be dry in no time at all, or at least dry enough to make a dash for it up the stairs of Taigh Blath to my room.'

'It is my pleasure,' he said, his voice low. Selina longed to narrow the gap between them, to feel his body pressed against hers, his arms wrapped around her, but she did not move. This was for the best, even if it meant awkwardness between them.

For a few minutes they sat in silence, watching the fire burn and listening to the sticks crackling in the heat. Selina felt mesmerised by the flames and at first she barely noticed the tickling sensation on her leg, only looking down when it moved a little higher. Curious, she lifted the hem of her petticoat only to feel a jolt of pure panic. A large spider was crawling up her leg, its body hairy and legs thick. She felt a wave of revulsion and screamed, frantically brushing her legs, hoping to send the spider falling to the ground.

Callum was by her side immediately and, sensing her terror, he gripped hold of her arms and held her until she calmed.

'It was only a little spider, lass,' he said, trying to keep the smile from his lips.

'That was far from little. It was a beast.'

'It's gone now. Scuttled back to wherever it came from.'

She looked suspiciously down at her legs, pulling the wet material of her petticoats up to inspect her knees.

From next to her she heard Callum groan. 'You're trying to bewitch me.'

She looked up indignantly, but saw the smile on his lips and relaxed.

'Scotland is a land of legends,' he said as she rearranged her petticoat, content that there were no more spiders lurking nearby. 'We have many creatures of myth, those that lure poor sailors or farmers to their doom.'

'You're comparing me to one of these creatures? I suppose you are meant to be the poor farmer boy?'

Callum laughed. 'No, but I do sometimes find myself wondering if you are some sort of selkie.'

'What is a selkie?'

'There are many interpretations, but in local folklore selkies are creatures that can take the shape of a seal or a human. They spend most of their time in the water, in their animal form, but once every seven years they can walk upon the land. They are said to be incredibly beautiful and enchant any human who comes across them.' He paused, his eyes flicking over her before he quickly looked away. 'Our stories tell of men obsessed by the selkie's beauty, stealing her sealskin so she cannot turn back into her animal form.' He cleared his throat and then looked at her again. 'You are beautiful, Selina. You have this radiance that shines from you. I find myself unable to look away.'

'For such a practical man that sounds very fanciful.'

It was a few seconds before he replied, his expression serious, 'I find I lose sight of huge parts of myself when I am with you.'

He held her gaze as wave upon wave of feeling passed between them. Slowly he moved towards her, his hand coming up to her cheek, his eyes searching hers.

'I know I cannot kiss you, yet I can think of nothing else.'

Selina swallowed hard. More than anything she wanted to surrender to the desire that pulsed inside her. She swayed slightly, her shoulder brushing his arm, allowing herself to imagine what might be if they put their own needs and desires first. It would be exquisite, yet even as she allowed herself to hope for one moment she knew it could not be. Callum would be giving up too much if he chose her over the promises he had made to his people.

'Callum,' she said quietly, taking his hand from her cheek and holding it tightly.

'I know,' he said, giving a tight smile.

They sat on the log side by side in silence for another ten minutes. Selina was acutely aware of Callum only a few inches away. Her body throbbed with anticipation, screaming at her to stop being so foolish and to reach out and take what she wanted. Surely it could not be too big a mistake to give in to the desire that was thrumming through her body, just once.

Even if she knew there was no future for them, at least then she would have the memories to sustain her.

Before she could reprimand herself for such foolish thoughts Hamish let out two low, controlled barks.

Callum stiffened, immediately on alert, and held a hand out to tell Selina to remain quiet.

Slowly he stood, his eyes darting to the left and right as he tried to work out what Hamish was barking at. Selina couldn't see anything, but after a moment Callum moved to stamp out the fire, and then took Selina by the hand and led her to a spot behind an old tree with a thick trunk.

She opened her mouth to whisper a question, but he anticipated her and shook his head before leaning in, his lips so close they brushed against her ear.

'There's two people about twenty feet away, walking through the forest.'

They stood, bodies pressed together, up against the tree trunk for what felt like an eternity. Only when Hamish came trotting up did either of them relax.

'Have they gone?' Selina whispered. 'Who was it? What did they want?'

Callum did not answer, taking his time to survey their surroundings. 'They've gone,' he said eventually. 'I could not see who it was, probably just two locals out for a walk.'

'You're sure they're gone.'

'Yes, we're safe.' He crouched down and stroked Hamish behind the ears. 'Good boy. There will be some chicken for you later tonight.'

'Thank goodness for Hamish.'

Selina's heart was still pounding in her chest and as Callum straightened she felt a rush of relief mixed with recklessness. She had nearly had her reputation ruined by being caught in the woods dressed only in a translucent chemise with the Earl of Leven. No one would care that they had actually been completely and utterly chaste.

Before she could stop herself she reached out and gripped Callum's shirt, pulling him towards her. She kissed him, long and hard, not letting go of his shirt until she felt his hand come up to cup her face.

'What are you doing, Selina?' he murmured when he pulled away.

'I am fed up with being sensible, following all the rules,' she said, knowing her words were madness. There was this rebellious part of her that wanted to experience what it felt like to have the man she loved make love to her, even if it was just once. Already they were risking so much, being out her in the woods together, she suddenly wanted to throw caution to the wind and take what she wanted.

She rose up on her tiptoes and kissed him again,

revelling in the warmth of his lips, loving the way he could not resist trailing his fingers over her skin.

'We shouldn't...'

'Do you want me, Callum?'

'Of course.'

'Then let us just enjoy this moment, without any expectation of another.' She kissed him again and felt the hardness in his trousers as he pressed against her. There was still a hint of hesitation, but as she drew him to her he groaned, unable to resist.

After a moment she pulled away and, holding his gaze, she slipped Callum's jacket from her shoulders, then gripped the hem of her chemise and lifted it up over her head. Never before had she done anything so brazen, but it was liberating just doing exactly what she wanted for once, without worrying about pleasing anyone else.

'You're beautiful,' he said, taking his time as he looked at her. 'I knew you were beautiful, but you're more than that. You're perfect.'

He closed the gap between them and kissed her again, his lips soft but insistent. As they kissed he trailed his fingertips down her naked back, stopping just at the top of her buttocks, then repeating the movement all over again. His touch was gentle, a mere caress, but as his fingers danced over her skin Selina felt her body begin to warm. Up until now she had felt in control of their encounter, but as he touched her she felt him take charge, now as fully invested in their dalliance as she was.

'You still have all your clothes on,' Selina whispered in between kisses. She felt disorientated, as if she had been swimming underwater for a while, that euphoric giddy sensation.

'You wish me to disrobe?'

'It seems only fair.'

'Your wish is my command, my lady.'

Callum kicked off his boots, coming back to kiss her before he pulled away and quickly unfastened his trousers and then lifted his shirt over his head.

Selina couldn't help herself. She stepped forward and laid her palms against the sculpted muscles of his chest, feeling the heat of him against her hands. She curled her fingers so her nails were resting against his skin and raked them gently down his torso. He let out a shuddering breath and then inhaled deeply.

'Are you sure you haven't done this before?' he murmured.

She smiled and shook her head, dipping lower with her hands so that she grazed the waistband of his trousers.

'I still think you've bewitched me. I feel like one of those Greek sailors, entranced by the beauty of the witch Circe, willing to do anything for one kiss.'

Selina moved in closer so her lips were touching his ear. 'You can have much more than one kiss.'

He took his kiss and then guided her over to the clearing, laying his jacket carefully on the ground for her. He ensured she was comfortable before giving her a wicked grin and then straddling her, leaning forward to kiss her soft skin. Selina gasped as he trailed his lips over her breasts, circling her nipples until she wanted to cry out. When he finally grazed one nipple with his teeth Selina groaned loudly. A jolt of pleasure shot through her body and she felt a pulse of warmth between her legs. Within a minute Selina was writhing underneath him as he nipped and sucked and kissed her breasts.

As she arched her back to meet him she let out a moan much louder than she meant to and they both froze at the sound. Selina squeezed her eyes tight, biting her lip, wondering if it had been as loud as she felt it was.

Neither moved for a minute and then another, and only when the woods remained silent after that did Callum move, pressing his lips close to her ear.

'Hush, my love.' It was an instruction, but also a challenge, and as he moved away, his body raking against hers, she knew he was going to make it very hard for her to keep quiet.

This time he did not stop at her breasts, but carried

on lower with his kisses. Instinctively she pressed her thighs together, only relaxing as he gently coaxed them apart. She gasped as his lips trailed lower and had to press the back of her hand against her mouth as he flicked his tongue against her most private place.

Selina was lost almost immediately. The sensation of Callum's lips on her and his fingers as they dipped inside her made her back arch and her breath come out in short pants. She never wanted him to stop, yet she did not know how much she could take. The tension built deep inside her until she felt a release and then wave after wave of pleasure coursing through her body.

Callum raised himself up and now Selina could see he had pushed off his trousers. While she was still in a haze of pleasure he held himself above her, until he was certain he had her full attention.

'We can stop if you want,' he murmured into her ear. 'It might kill me, but we can stop.'

In answer she pressed her hips up against his and felt him slip inside her. At first he moved slowly, giving her time to adjust, but as her body began to respond, her hips moving in time with his, he started to move faster until they found the perfect rhythm, their bodies coming together over and over again.

Selina felt the pressure building again and this time she did cry out, the sound cutting through the quiet woods until she buried her face in Callum's shoulder. As she felt her muscles tense and pulse, Callum stiffened, too, his head thrown back in ecstasy.

Callum held himself above her for a minute while Selina regained control of her senses, then ever so gently he moved off, collapsing back on to the ground beside her.

It took a long time for Selina to drift back down to earth and as she did she felt suffused with a warmth and satisfaction that she was not expecting. Even as she had initiated their intimacy she had wondered if she would regret it once it was over, but instead she was lying here feeling satisfied.

She knew nothing had changed, not really. Callum was still destined to marry Catherine and Selina was due to leave Scotland in a mere few weeks. Their futures hadn't altered, but she had allowed herself a sliver of happiness, something to hold on to while she made the long journey south to her new life.

'That was unexpected,' Callum said, his voice gruff. Selina turned to face him, aware they were both lying naked in the middle of the forest, but unable to summon the strength to get up.

'Certainly unplanned,' Selina said, 'But perhaps not unexpected. It has felt like an inevitability ever since we first shared a kiss.'

'Perhaps,' he said, a smile lingering on his lips for

a moment before it was replaced with a frown. She knew he was thinking of what happened next, of the weight of responsibility he now felt for her as well as his promise to the people of Ballachulish. She felt the first flicker of sadness threaten to ruin the warmth and happiness of a few moments earlier. She did not want to think about the future, about the time when Callum would stand at the altar and say his vows to another woman. She knew their intimacy did not change anything, not really, yet even though she had told herself she would not get possessive she felt stirrings of jealousy.

'We should get dressed, before anyone else happens upon us.'

As Selina stood Callum's eyes raked over her body and she wondered momentarily whether she could sink back down on to his soft jacket and pretend the rest of the world did not exist.

'You're right,' Callum said, not moving. 'Then we need to talk about what happens next.'

Selina stiffened for a moment, then shook her head. 'Nothing happens next,' she said as she pulled on her chemise and petticoats.'

'Of course it does. I am not without honour, I would not…'

Selina shook her head firmly. 'It changes nothing, Callum.'

She did not want to discuss it, to draw out the pain any further than necessary. Quickly she took her dress and slipped it on, reaching round behind her to do up the fastenings as best she could on her own.

Callum was on his feet now, pulling on his own clothes.

'Of course it changes things.'

'No,' Selina said firmly.

She suddenly felt completely overwhelmed. She did not want to argue with Callum, to have to tell him why a union between them would be doomed from the start. He had made his promise long before she had ever met him, she would not be the reason he let his people down. What was more, she did not want to be a burden, a duty he resented as the years went by. Better to take her happy memories and leave. In time Callum's face would grow hazy in her mind, she would never forget him, but she might be able to find happiness without him when the pain of these last few weeks faded.

'Goodbye, Callum,' she whispered, then turned on her heel and ran, not stopping until she reached the road. Only then did she check behind her, hating how much her heart was breaking as she realised Callum was not following her.

Chapter Seventeen

To Selina it felt as though she were in a dream world. The memories of half an hour earlier were fresh and vivid and she could not help but think about them every time her clothes brushed against her skin. It was as though she had been sleep-walking through life, unaware of the pleasures it could bring, yet now she was uncertain if she would ever get to experience those pleasures again.

'It's for the best,' Selina told herself as she marched briskly down the road. She was heading back to Taigh Blath. She would pack her bags and then ask her father for the funds to pay for her passage south. It would be a shock, her leaving so suddenly, but she did not think her father would object to her quitting his life for good.

The morning was still warm, although there were a few clouds gathering in the sky, but as Selina walked she found the fabric of her dress was still a little damp and made her shiver despite the mild temperatures.

She made it to the outskirts of the village without mishap and slowly she started to feel a little more like herself. The interlude in the woods with Callum had a dreamlike quality to it and she could half-persuade herself it had been merely a fantasy. Perhaps it was safer to think of it that way.

'Please, no. Please just give us more time.' A woman's voice cut through the silence of the morning. She sounded distraught and as Selina rounded the corner she saw a middle-aged woman clinging on to the arm of a young man. The man was stony faced, the only hint of emotion a little sneer pulling at his top lip. As she hurried closer she realised she had seen the man before. He was Mr Robertson, the local land steward who managed the estate and tenants for Sir William while he was in England. Mr Robertson had been to Taigh Blath a few times, discussing business and advising Sir William on the value of the land and the most reliable tenants.

Alongside the middle-aged woman were five children of varying ages, from a toddler who clung to her mother's skirts to a young teenager with fists clenched, being held back by his younger siblings.

'Please, just another few weeks. I'll get the money.'

Mr Robertson shrugged the woman's hand from his arm and towered menacingly above her.

'No more chances. You're out today. Sir William isn't running a charity.'

A small crowd had gathered and a neighbour stepped forward, gently pulling the woman away. She turned to Mr Robertson. 'You'll give Mrs Murray time to gather her belongings. Legally they belong to her, Sir William can't touch them.'

'Half an hour. After that I take the key and lock the door. Anything left behind will be forfeit.'

Mr Robertson took a seat on the low dry-stone wall that ran around the property, crossing his arms in front of his body. He gave her a curious look as she passed him, but said nothing.

Selina hesitated on the threshold of the cottage, not wanting to intrude at such a difficult time, but she had not been able to walk past without at least seeing if she could be of some assistance. She was facing her own troubles, but it was nothing compared to this mother of five being thrown out into the street with her children.

'Excuse me,' she said to the neighbour. 'I couldn't help but overhear what was happening. Is there anything I can do to help?'

The woman looked her up and down and then nodded.

'You're that young lass from Taigh Blath.'

Selina waited, wondering if she was about to be sent away.

'You're the one Lord Leven is sweet on, not the one he's meant to marry.' She shrugged. 'I've always thought him a good judge. If you're serious about helping, go upstairs and gather the children's clothes. They all have a spare set, their church clothes. We can carry them next door.'

Selina moved quickly, aware of the minutes ticking by for this family. To lose their home would be bad enough, to lose their meagre possessions as well would be devastating.

Upstairs there was another woman whom Selina recognised from the dance in the barn a few nights earlier and had been one of the women in the crowd outside. She was dashing around the two upstairs rooms, collecting what she could and placing it into the middle of a sheet that had been laid out on the floor. Selina joined her, working silently as she quickly collected and folded all the clothes she could find into a neat pile. She started with the children's, counting the outfits and undergarments out to make sure she wasn't missing any, and then moved on to Mrs Murray's. It felt good to be doing something for someone else, to forget her own troubles for a while.

* * *

Within twenty minutes the house had been cleared, the possessions taken away and stored in various neighbours' houses. Mrs Murray was escorted, weeping, out of the cottage and Selina followed.

Outside she saw a familiar figure striding up. Callum's face was like thunder, his expression fixed into a deep frown and his eyes flashing with barely concealed ire. He spoke to Mrs Murray quietly, nodding at her tear-choked answers and then moved to Mr Robertson.

Selina was torn, intrigued as to what he was saying to Mr Robertson, but also aware she did not want Callum to say anything foolish that might give away their intimacy earlier in the morning.

'I have my orders,' Mr Robertson said, raising his hands in front of him as if trying to ward off a bad spirit.

'Sir William instructed you to do this?'

'Mrs Murray has not paid her rent. His orders are to be tough on anyone even a day late. He wants an example made.'

'She has five children.'

'I'm merely doing my job. Don't make me out to be a heartless bastard. If I don't evict her, Sir William will just find someone else to do it.'

'And you approached this in a kind and gentle manner?' Callum asked, raising an eyebrow.

Mr Robertson had the decency the look away, his cheeks flushing. 'If I am not stern with them, people think they can take liberties. I have to be respected, feared even, to do my job.'

'You'll let her have a final check of the place, ensure nothing has been left behind?'

Mr Robertson nodded, watching as Callum approached the evicted woman.

'I am sorry this has happened,' Callum said. 'I understand Sir William's orders are final, but Mr Robertson has said you may have a little more time to check the house over before he takes the keys. I will speak with Sir William today, appeal to his sense of charity. I cannot promise to work miracles, but I will speak on your behalf.'

'Thank you, my lord,' Mrs Murray said, the tears streaming down her cheeks.

Selina stood back out of the way as the older woman stepped into her home for the last time, walking round the tiny cottage and checking all nooks and crannies for any precious forgotten items. Only once she re-emerged and was swept away by one of the neighbours for a fortifying cup of tea did Callum approach Selina.

'You were helping Mrs Murray?' he said, touching her lightly on the arm. Out here in public there could be no more obvious sign of affection, but she felt her treacherous heart flutter all the same. 'You ran away so quickly from the woods I thought I might not catch you.'

'I was passing when Mr Robertson arrived to remove her from the house. I cannot believe anyone could be so callous. She has five children.'

'She is a widow. I understand she takes in laundry for other people and her eldest son has started as a farm labourer on one of the larger farms a few miles away, but the family does not have much income.' Callum shook his head in disgust. 'Mr Robertson is only doing the job given to him, although he is a spiteful man and no doubt thrives in his work. It is Sir William who has given the orders.'

'These are the people you wish to help,' Selina said, her gaze fixed on the dilapidated little row of cottages. Sir William might be quick to demand a late payment, but it did not look as though he did much to maintain the ramshackle building.

'Yes. Before my father died the Thomson family owned these cottages and dozens more like them scattered through the village and local area. They were sold to cover my father's debt and I lost the ability to be a more understanding landlord.' Callum grimaced. 'My father was many things—irresponsible, a drunkard, a fool—but he was not an unfair landlord. He pretty much left people alone, didn't raise rents unfairly. Sometimes it took a bit of prompting for him to do the work needed to maintain the properties he owned, but the tenants could see his lack of interest was of benefit to them on the whole.'

'This is what you wish to regain control of, alongside Taigh Blath and the grounds.'

'Yes. All over the Highlands good people are being thrown from their homes and their farms for the sake of a few pounds of annual profit. It is becoming more profitable for the landowners to turn their land to sheep, rather than have all these disconnected smaller tenant farmers. Whole communities are being destroyed and I don't want that to happen to Ballachulish.'

She glanced around her, checking no one else could hear what she had to say next.

'*This* is why we cannot be together, Callum. I finally understand the human impact of it, the awful suffering people are going through because Sir William is in control of their lives. I know you have been telling me the same, over and over for weeks, but I do understand now.'

'You cannot be serious,' he said, gripping her arm and leading her a little further away from the cottage. 'There is no other option after what we did today. We will marry.'

'No,' she said firmly and much louder than she meant to. With great effort she managed to regain control of herself and lowered her voice. 'No, Callum. I will not be the reason you break your vow to these people. It will eat away at both of us and we will be miserable. As the years go by and you see your people suffering you will come to resent me.' She took a great shuddering breath. 'I love you, Callum, but I will not be a mistake you made that changed the course of your life.'

He blinked quickly, as if he could not understand what she was saying.

Selina pushed on, willing him to accept what she was saying. 'I deserve more than your regret.'

'Selina, you cannot seriously think we could do anything other than marry, not after today.'

She exhaled slowly and shook her head. 'I need a bath and a lie down, Callum. My head is spinning. Let us talk tomorrow. In the meantime, think what it is you truly want, for I think deep in your heart I come second.'

Before he could answer she walked away, knowing he could not chase after her out here in public. It took all her effort not to break down into tears and, as she walked towards Taigh Blath, she wondered if she would ever feel happiness again.

Chapter Eighteen

More than anything Selina wished to slip into Taigh Blath undetected and run up the stairs to her room. The morning had been emotionally exhausting and the last thing she needed was to have to pretend to her stepmother or half-sister that everything was well.

As the front door was opened by a footman Selina's heart sank. Catherine was walking through the hall and she paused as Selina stepped inside.

'Oh, good, Mother has been looking for you. It is time for lunch.'

'I might just go and change first,' Selina said, aware her dress was crumpled from being put back on damp.

'No need,' Catherine said sharply, taking Selina's arm. 'You never look nice anyway.' She marched Selina to the dining room and pushed her in through the door. Selina wondered at Catherine's behaviour, but it had been such a strange day she thought perhaps she was making too much of her half-sister's coldness.

'Good afternoon,' she said quietly as she entered the dining room. She glanced at her father, aware that her recent actions were not going to enhance her relationship with the man. She had made her peace with moving on, had decided to give up on seeking his affection, but she could not completely let go of the hope that he might tell her she mattered to him.

'You look terrible,' Lady Kingsley announced, pushing her chair back from the table. 'I do hope you are not getting ill. You're rather a sickly young woman and I do not wish to catch anything from you.'

Selina gave a bland smile. Lady Kingsley's sharp tongue was spiteful, but she now let the words just bounce off her.

'I don't think that's why she is looking exhausted,' Catherine said, pouring herself a cup of tea.

'She can hardly claim her days are filled with exertion or hard labour. An honest day's work would be a shock to her.' Lady Kingsley chuckled at the idea.

Sir William raised a hand, frowning. He did not normally intervene when his wife and daughter were sniping at Selina, but he did not like conflict at the dining table. 'Let us enjoy this meal in peace. It will be one of the last we have all together, with Catherine leaving us for Lord Leven's table in a few short weeks.'

'You have finalised the contract?' Lady Kingsley said, her interest piqued. Although she clearly loved Catherine, she had ambition like her husband. She wanted her daughter to marry well and would leverage any advantage that brought her to climb a few rungs further up the social ladder.

'Nearly.'

'What do you think of the marriage, Selina?' Catherine said, her voice sharp. 'Surely you must have something to say about it all as my wedding day draws closer.'

The question came as a surprise. Catherine normally did her utmost to avoid having to talk to Selina and this morning she seemed especially prickly, so Selina couldn't work out what her motivation for engaging was.

Taking a long sip of tea, Selina tried to buy herself some time. She did not want to be disingenuous, but equally she could not tell the truth. Announcing she had spent a wonderfully intimate morning with the man Catherine was going to marry would hardly be a good way to ensure Sir William gave her the money she needed to travel south.

'I want you to be happy,' Selina said, choosing her words carefully. It was not a lie. She did not hate

Catherine and could sympathise with the difficult position she was in, a pawn in her father's machinations to climb higher in Society, even if she did share those ambitions.

'That is sweet. You want me to be happy with Lord Leven?'

Selina glanced at her half-sister, trying to ascertain the motive behind the words.

'I want you to be happy whatever your future holds.'

'Surely you think my future holds a marriage to Lord Leven?'

'Of course.'

'A long and happy marriage to Lord Leven?'

Selina swallowed hard, bringing her eyes up to meet Catherine's and as their gaze met it was clear that Catherine knew. There was a simmering hatred in her eyes along with a sliver of hurt.

'Tell me,' Catherine said, her nose crinkling in disdain. 'You've always craved a position in this family. I've always thought it pathetic how you paw and fawn at *my* father, acting as though he owes you something just because twenty-two years ago your whore of a mother couldn't keep her legs closed...'

'Catherine,' Lady Kingsley exclaimed, a hand flying to her mouth. Sir William was silent, his eyes narrowed, as if aware there was something deeper, something important, going on here. He was an observant man and he merely shifted in his seat, watching how things would play out.

'Did you think committing the ultimate betrayal would be a good way to earn my father's affection?'

'Catherine...' Selina said, her expression pleading. Desperately she tried to work out how Catherine could know what had happened in the woods. Surely no one had seen them.

'You do know he has only tolerated you for this long because of the damage you could do to his reputation if you were to make your sordid claims about your parenthood public. You are nothing more than a dirty little secret that doesn't have the good sense to see when she is not wanted. You are worthless in this world.'

Selina felt the tears prick at her eyes, but refused to let these people see her cry. This past year she had felt worthless, like a dirty little secret.

She stood, thinking it best to remove herself from this situation. She would go upstairs and pack a bag and then perhaps find a way to speak to her father alone. No more did she want to be a pawn in other people's lives, moved around without a say in what her future held.

'Sit down,' Sir William said, his tone brooking no argument.

Selina hesitated but then retook her seat.

'I think you had better tell us what is going on, Catherine,' Sir William said, his eyes fixed on Selina.

'Ever since we arrived in Scotland she has been scheming. I've seen her acting inappropriately with Lord Leven, touching his arm as she giggles at whatever amusing thing he has to say.'

Selina opened her mouth to protest, but was silenced by a warning hand from her father.

'It was horrible to watch, but I told myself it didn't really matter. Lord Leven is an earl. He knows breeding. A nobody like Selina is fine for a flirtation, but he would not taint his bloodline with her.'

'I told you we should have pushed her back in the gutter the very day she came begging at our door,' Lady Kingsley said, looking at Selina with pure hatred in her eyes.

'A noise in the middle of the night woke me from sleep and I could not settle. I rose and thought I might get some milk from the kitchens. As I was going downstairs I saw Lord Leven sneaking out. He hadn't been visiting me in the middle of the night, so there was only one possible place he could have come from.' She cleared her throat. 'And this is after I saw him sneaking from the house after the ball. Selina assured me he had escorted her home, nothing more, but that was clearly a lie.'

Selina felt the awful irony of the situation. Last night she had sent Callum away with nothing more than a kiss. Yet it had been that indiscretion that caught them out, not the one in the woods.

'See, she does not deny it. The little whore has been caught entertaining my future husband in the middle of the night.'

Out of the corner of her eye Selina watched her father. For half a minute he remained very still, not even blinking. He looked like a statue, although not one Selina would want in her home. Then slowly he rose to his feet, his eyes still fixed on her, but his top lip quivering with rage.

'Is this true?'

The sensible thing to do would be to flee. Sir William was angrier than she had ever seen him before and all of that anger was directed towards her. Yet Selina could not have moved if a hundred petrified elephants were stampeding her way. She felt mesmerised, frozen to the spot, unable to do anything except wait and see how things unfolded.

'Is. This. True?' His words were clipped, each syllable filled with rage, and a cold trickle of fear ran through her. She wondered if she was in physical danger. Sir William could lash out and no one in this room would be inclined to stop him.

With a quick glance to the door, she stood and then squared her shoulders as she faced her father.

'Yes.'

The room was completely silent, each second stretching out for an eternity.

'After everything I have done for you. The months of housing you, feeding you, clothing you. Bringing you to Scotland with my family.' He stalked out around the table so he was standing directly in front of her, towering over her petite form.

Selina stood firm, despite her instinct to run. For months she had suffered the emotional manipulation at the hands of this man. Every so often there would be a glimmer of affection or appreciation, always when she was close to giving up her aim of becoming closer to her father. It had been a horrible cycle, always keeping her hanging on, driving her away and then pulling her back.

'I am your daughter,' she said, raising her chin. Inside her chest her heart was beating so fast she was afraid it might give out and she was having to take shallow, shaky breaths, but she did not back away from her father.

'You knew I existed all those years, but you never gave my poor mother any assistance. You let her raise two children by herself, disgraced and driven away from her family. She might have been a foolish young girl when you met her, ready to believe your promises, your lies, but you knew what you were doing.' She poked a finger in his chest, surprised at her own bravery. 'I owe you nothing, Sir William.'

He spluttered and blustered before rallying and gripping her by the arm, his fingers digging into her flesh.

'You will get nothing more from me. Not a single penny, not anything to help towards your journey home. I do not care if you starve on the streets or die in a ditch. Leave here and never come back.'

He thrust her in front of him, pushing her out of the dining room and into the hall. Catherine and Lady Kingsley watched with a mixture of horror and satisfaction on their faces. Sir William wrenched open the front door and pushed her bodily outside.

'You have five minutes to get off my property or I will send every single one of my servants and employees to chase you off.'

'What about my things?'

'I will burn them for you.'

Selina swallowed hard, thinking of the letters from Sarah and the few personal possessions she had accumulated over the time she had spent with the Kingsleys. She cared not about the clothes, other than to realise it might be a while before she was able to change out of her current dress.

With as much dignity as she could muster Selina turned and began to walk steadily away from the house. More than anything she wanted to break out into a run, but she could feel her father's eyes on her back and she did not want to give him the satisfaction of seeing her affected so much.

Chapter Nineteen

'Sir William knows,' Selina said as she burst through the door of the little cottage, the words tumbling from her mouth as if they could not be contained any longer.

She paused, looking around her. It was not a large house, but inside was beautifully decorated and Callum had chosen pieces of well-made, simple furniture. Everything was spotlessly clean and Selina felt a sense of safety here she had not experienced for a long time. She shook herself; now was not time to start imagining herself mistress of this home.

'He knows…?'

'About us. About last night. Catherine was awake early and saw you leaving. She thinks we were intimate then and she told her father.'

'But we weren't…'

'Not then,' Selina agreed, 'But it hardly matters, does it? You were seen creeping out of Taigh Blath and even though at that point we had not...' She waved her hands around, suddenly embarrassed to put what they had done in the woods into words, 'They know you have taken my virtue.'

Callum staggered back, flopping into the comfortable armchair set in front of the fireplace.

'She told Sir William this morning and I could not deny it. He called me all sorts and then escorted me from the house.'

'He threw you out?'

Selina nodded. 'As I am. I did not have much with me, and the clothes in my trunk were mainly ones he had bought me over the past year, but he did not even allow me time to gather my sentimental items.'

'He is a cold man.'

All the tears Selina had desperately tried not to shed in front of her father welled up now and spilled on to her cheeks.

'I hate him,' she said quietly. 'All this time I have been desperate for his love, for some attention from him, yet he is a monster. What does that make me?'

'A young woman who wanted to know her father, nothing more.'

Callum reached out and took Selina's hand.

'You're not alone, Selina,' he said, his tone reassuring.

She looked at him long and hard, her eyes flicking over his face, trying to work out what he was thinking.

'I am alone,' she said eventually. Despite being thrown out of Taigh Blath, nothing had changed, not really.

'You're not alone. I would not abandon you after what we did in the woods…'

'So I am an obligation?'

Callum stiffened, realising he was on shaky ground. His mind was whirring and he perhaps wasn't being his most sensitive, yet it was hard to concentrate on just Selina when he had the guilt of the thought of abandoning the people of Ballachulish to their fate with Sir William. A now irate Sir William.

'No, not an obligation. I meant what I said last night, Selina, I love you.'

She studied him again and he felt as though somehow she was slipping away from him. He had struggled to understand her vehement refusal to marry him. After they had made love he had thought the decision was made. He would not walk away from a woman who could be pregnant with his child. When Selina had told him nothing had changed, that she still meant to leave Scotland and he should still marry Catherine, he had been stunned.

'What do you propose for our future?' she asked, a sharp edge to her voice. 'We marry and stay in Ballachulish and watch Sir William destroy the lives of everyone you have ever cared about.'

'I...'

'I finally see, Callum. I mean really understand. Seeing Mrs Murray pleading with that horrible Mr Robertson, her life destroyed in an instant, her children gathered round to see her humiliation...it was awful.'

'I know,' Callum said quietly.

'Many men would be able to live with that. They have hard hearts and a self-interest that is at the forefront of what they do, but not you.' Selina's voice was softer now, but the tears were still flowing. 'It would destroy you, seeing the people of Ballachulish evicted from their homes one by one, the community decimated, the villagers scattered to wherever they could get work and shelter.'

'That doesn't mean I will ignore my duty to you.'

Selina wailed, 'I don't want to be a duty. For a year I have been a burden, a dirty little secret to be hidden away and controlled and suppressed at every opportunity. I have become a shell of my former self. I doubt my sister would recognise me if she passed me on the street and she certainly would be puzzled at what I have let myself become. I have spirit, I have a backbone. I am not some simpering girl who is content with being ordered around. Yet this past year I have allowed Sir William to turn me into something I am not. Weak.'

'I don't think you're weak, Selina. I think you're one of the strongest young women I've ever met.'

'I will be,' she said, her voice low and determined.

'You are not merely a duty,' he said carefully, not wanting to lose this point. 'I love you, Selina.'

A soft smile flickered on to her lips. 'I know. It baffles me, but I know you love me.' She sighed and took up the empty seat opposite him and for a long moment they were both silent. He could sense her mind whirring, her eyes flicking from side to side. All he wanted to do was reach out and touch her, to caress her face and show her he did care for her.

'I might not be merely a duty, but there is a sense of doing the right thing when you look at me. I don't want that, Callum. I want to be all anyone can think about. I want someone to be completely and unreservedly happy to marry me, not conflicted about it.' She held up her hand to quiet his protest. 'You cannot have everything you wish for. Either you marry me and the people you care about suffer, or you let me go and you can salvage the situation with Sir William.'

'I will not let you go. There has to be some other way.'

Selina shook her head sadly. 'I am not asking you to choose, Callum. I am making the decision for us.'

'You're saying no to a life with me.'

'I'm saying no to making you miserable.'

'You wouldn't make me miserable.'

'What you lost by marrying me would.' She sighed. 'And as I said, it is not just about you. I am finished with being an inconvenience, I do not want to be hidden or explained away. It might sound selfish, but I want to be *the* most important thing in someone's life.'

'Selina…'

She shook her head. 'My mind is made up, Callum. I will not spend my life feeling responsible for so many people's unhappiness. And I will not marry you knowing you might grow to resent me in the years that come.'

'I could never resent you, Selina.'

Callum felt a deep desperation. He had never really considered how he had made Selina feel these last few weeks. He'd been unable to hide his attraction to her, unable to keep himself from kissing her, yet all the time he had shown her that she was not his priority. No wonder she was so reluctant now to believe him when he said they could have a future together. She had been conditioned over the last year, a terrible year spent with her cruel father, to believe she was not worth anything—the last thing he wanted to do was reinforce that idea.

'Please, will you just give me a little time? I need to—'

'No,' she said quickly. 'You are a very persuasive man, Lord Leven, and if I stay here in Ballachulish for too long you will no doubt convince me of anything you want.' She bit her lip. 'I do have a favour to ask though, the main reason I came here today. I have no funds whatsoever. I wonder if you could lend me the money for a passage back to England. I know my sister will give me the money to pay you back as soon as I turn up on her doorstep and I will send it with haste.'

'You're leaving for England.'

'I think it is for the best, Callum.'

'How can it be for the best if we are never to see one another again?'

'You are a persuasive man, a charming one when you want to be. Go and use that charm on Sir William and Catherine. Conspire with them on this story that I am a fallen woman, a seductress, and you are merely a man who was unable to resist some physical gratification.'

'What we have is so much more than that,' he said, feeling the anger begin to swell inside him. 'You may want to brush away everything we have shared, but I do not.'

'For the sake of your people, you need for me to be the common enemy. Catherine will forgive you when she realises your story agrees with her narrative—she is the valuable daughter, I am good only for a short fling. She will ask her father to forgive you and to proceed with the marriage. Negotiate hard, regain control of what your father lost to debt and give the people of Ballachulish the landlord they deserve.'

'You make it sound so easy,' he muttered. Inside his chest he was feeling a tight squeeze and he wondered if this was what it felt like to have your heart broken.

Selina stood and bent over his chair, kissing him lightly on the lips. 'It is not easy, not for either of us, but it is for the best.'

She turned and walked over to the door. 'I will take a room at the Lost Sheep for the night. If you could arrange for someone to bring me the money to pay for my fare to London, I will start on my journey tomorrow. I am sure the innkeeper will know the best way to seek passage south.'

Callum stood, launching himself forward to grab her arm as she turned to go. Firmly he pulled her towards him and kissed her long and hard. His mind was reeling and he didn't agree with anything she had said, but he needed time to work out how to get himself out of this mess and convince Selina not to leave.

Chapter Twenty

Selina kept to her room at the Lost Sheep, despite its tiny size and lack of comfortable furniture. There was a small wooden chair in one corner alongside a narrow bed with a straw mattress. A tiny window let in some natural light, but also a persistent draught that made her shiver despite the mild temperatures.

Downstairs there was a fire burning in the main room, making it smoky and dark, but the landlord had also shown her a private area for guests staying in the rooms above the Lost Sheep's bar which was a little more comfortable. Despite this option Selina preferred to stay upstairs where she could cry in peace.

Callum had not been expecting anything she had said that afternoon, that much had been clear. He'd been blindsided by the news that Sir William knew about the night Callum had crept into Taigh Blath. As Selina thought about it more she wondered if in truth it was a blessing in disguise. Callum would have tried hard to make everything work, to keep everyone happy, but there was no way to balance marrying her with regaining control of the tenancies for the people of Ballachulish. No one would be completely contented and Callum would bear the weight of his own disappointment for the rest of their lives.

At least this way it was quick and clean. She was finally out from under the influence of her horrible father and his true family and she would not have to watch as Callum destroyed himself with regret.

Selina choked back a sob as she thought about not seeing his smile again, at not feeling his lips on hers. She thought of the soft, Scottish accent as he whispered endearments in her ear and nuzzled at her neck. Despite her certainty that she was doing the right thing, she felt completely and utterly heartbroken. Yet she knew she was right.

Her sister, Sarah, was more reserved than Selina, but in her letters Selina could read between the lines and understand the love Sarah and her husband shared. It was there in the little gestures Sarah mentioned. Their love was unconditional and unfettered and Selina had finally realised that was what she wanted. After a year of basically begging for affection from a man who would rather she did not exist, she was not about to fall into another relationship where she was a disappointment. Callum would never say that he regretted their marriage, but she would be able to see it each and every day as he watched the villagers he thought of as *his people* be turned from their homes.

Footsteps sounded in the corridor outside and then there was a short, sharp knock on the door.

Selina opened it quickly, thinking it might be someone Callum had sent with the money for her trip home, but was surprised to find Lady Kingsley standing outside, looking around in disgust.

'Come on, quickly, girl. Let me in.'

Selina opened the door wide to allow her stepmother into the room. Once inside Lady Kingsley cast around in disdain before deciding to settle for the wooden chair. She perched on the very edge as if worried she might catch something if she relaxed too much.

Refusing to stand on ceremony for her stepmother, Selina sat on the bed and waited for Lady Kingsley to speak.

'Abandoned by the man that made you a whore already? This is quite the hovel you find yourself in.'

Selina didn't react, just sat waiting for Lady Kingsley to get to the point. There was no need for politeness any longer, now she wasn't living under the Kingsleys' roof, and she wasn't going to waste small talk on a woman she despised.

Lady Kingsley cleared her throat. 'I have an offer for you. I suggest you take it.'

'What is the offer?'

'I will give you the money for the journey home. A gift, no need to repay it.'

Selina's eyes widened with surprise. 'And in return?' There had to be a catch to this bargain, something Lady Kingsley would benefit from, otherwise she would not be here.

'In return you leave Ballachulish today and make your journey in haste back to England.'

In silence Selina considered the offer, trying to work out her stepmother's motivations.

'What is more, you never contact me or my husband or my daughter ever again.'

'That would be my pleasure,' Selina murmured.

'You agree to the bargain?'

Selina cocked her head to the side and considered the older woman in front of her. This day should be triumphant for her. Ever since Selina had turned up at Sir William's door, Lady Kingsley had been trying to get rid of her. Never had she defied her husband's orders to keep Selina close in case she let slip her true identity as Sir William's illegitimate daughter, but she had been especially cruel, hoping to drive Selina away.

'You are hoping to salvage this marriage between

Catherine and Lord Leven,' Selina said quietly. It could be the only reason for this sudden show of generosity.

'I do. He's an earl. An impoverished one, but an earl all the same. And he's hardly the first man who has had trouble resisting a little easy temptation. Catherine will forgive him and in time it will be as though you never existed.'

Even though this was what Selina had been pushing for earlier in the day, for her to return to England and Callum to continue with the original plan and marry Catherine, the idea of them together still stung. Callum wouldn't forget her, not easily. At least not for a year or maybe two, but in ten years' time she would be a distant memory, nothing more than a mistake he had nearly made.

'Will Sir William agree?'

'Of course. He's angry now, but that anger can be moulded to be directed towards you. It is an easy story to tell: the harlot, the temptress, the illegitimate daughter who was raised without morals.' Lady Kingsley's lip curled back in disgust as she spoke, revealing her long, polished teeth. 'By the time I'm finished he will be reminded that men cannot be held responsible for their desires, that it is only natural, positive even, for a hot-blooded male to bed whomever he wants. It is a very separate thing to marriage.'

Her father would accept this narrative; to do anything else would be the ultimate hypocrisy given how he had seduced Selina's mother, waited until she was pregnant and then disappeared.

'I don't doubt he will make Lord Leven sweat, perhaps threaten to withhold some of his precious land from the dowry and marriage agreement, but in the end he will concede.' Lady Kingsley laughed, a high, brittle sound that whistled as she sucked air through her pursed lips. 'What use is this land to him? It provides a few measly pounds here and there in rents, but he has to employ a local to manage it. It was always a means to an end. A way to leverage a better position in Society.'

'Sir William does not want the land here?'

'No. What he wants is his rightful place among the *ton* and a lovely fertile parcel of land down in Sussex or somewhere respectable.'

At least Callum would get back his ancestral lands and ownership of the farms and cottages around the village. It was what she had pushed him towards this afternoon, what she hoped would make him happy.

'We have a deal,' Selina said. Normally she would not take money from Lady Kingsley, but she thought it was best if she left Ballachulish as quickly as possible. No doubt Callum still thought there was some way he could restore his family's lands and not lose her, but she was more realistic. The more distance she put between Callum and herself the easier it would be to stick to her plan.

'We will never see or hear from you again.'

'Never.'

'I do not wish for you to turn up in six months, begging for more money.'

Selina raised an eyebrow. 'It was never about the money, Lady Kingsley. My sister, my true sister, Sarah, is married to a viscount and she is the most generous person you could ever meet. I plan to make my own way in the world, but even if I fall on hard times she would not see me asking our horrible father for a single penny.'

Without another word Lady Kingsley reached into her reticule and pulled out some money, carefully counting it before handing it over.

'Leave today. Even if you only get as far as the next village before sundown. I want you out of Ballachulish.'

The older woman stood to leave, sweeping from the room with her chin tilted high just in case Selina had forgotten that her stepmother was far too good for these surroundings.

'Give my best wishes to Catherine in her marriage,' Selina called out.

Lady Kingsley did not look back, but called loudly enough for Selina to hear, 'Leave. Today.'

Callum was back in the woods just outside Ballachulish. It was a place of peace and serenity, somewhere he had always come to think. After his father's death he had spent hours wandering this woodland, occasionally glimpsing the blue expanse of the loch nearby, trying to make the difficult decisions that needed to be made. Here he was again, over a decade later, still plagued by uncertainty.

He walked up a steep trail through the trees, enjoying the burn in the muscles of his legs and the thumping of his heart in his chest. He always had found activity helped him to focus, to think. It was why he enjoyed Bruce's invitations to throw knives or axes in the woods. It meant his head was clear and his mind sharp.

Today, though, his emotions were too overwhelming to get any sort of clarity. He walked briskly until he came out at the top of the hill, the bank falling away sharply in front of him to give a clear view of the sparkling water. This was his home, his land. His mother had always joked that if you cut him open you would find the soil of the Highlands all the way through him. In the years of his exile—for it had felt like an exile, a punishment for not being able to save his ancestral lands—he had longed for the sweet air of the mountains and the cool waters of the lochs. When he had first set foot back on Scottish soil he had felt as though a piece of himself had been restored.

As he stood looking out over the shimmering waters of the loch he felt something new, a longing that was not solely focused on his ancestral lands. There was an emptiness in his heart that he had never felt before when up here.

'I can't do this without her,' he murmured to himself. Whatever happened, whatever the future held, he did not want to be facing it without Selina.

Yet he knew he would never forgive himself if he put his own needs and desires above those of the people relying on him. Surely the right decision was one that benefited the most people. He needed to save the people of Ballachulish from...

His thought trailed off as his mind fixed on one word. *Save.* As it circled again and again round his mind he felt it didn't sound quite right. The people who lived and worked on the tenant farms and rented houses from Sir William looked to him for leadership, but they had never asked him to save them. It was something his mother had tried to gently point out time and again over the years. He did not need to be their saviour. They were people with complex lives.

Yes, he could make things better for them by regaining control of the land and being a fair landlord, but they had never asked him to *save* them.

Callum leaned forward, resting his hands on his thighs and sucking in great gulps of air. He felt suddenly sick, looking back at his actions over the years in a new light. The light that everyone else must view things in. He saw himself as a young man, barely more than a boy, grieving the father he had a complicated relationship with, struggling to come to terms with the mountain of debt his inheritance was under.

The decision he'd made that day, to sell the estate, had been inescapable, but even now more than a decade on he still felt a pang of guilt every time he thought of it. Of course, there had been no other option. It was either sell or let the creditors come and seize what they wanted. At least by selling he had been able to provide his mother with her little cottage, a home to call her own while he sought his fortune in Canada.

Even his years in Canada had been plagued by guilt. Every moment of every day he had carried the faces of the people of Ballachulish, the men and women whom he felt a great responsibility for. He had pored over every letter, desperate for news, blaming himself when a family had to move away or were struck by some tragedy. His focus on making enough money to start the process of buying back some of the land he had lost had been all-consuming and now Callum wondered if it was completely healthy.

Since his return to Scotland, and his negotiations with Sir William, he had felt there was a sliver of hope. The possibility that he might regain what he had lost had been addictive and he had barrelled down the proposed path without really thinking. For once his overriding emotion had not been guilt, but hope, and it was much better than the alternative. In his mind he saw a way to redeem himself, to redeem his family.

Callum straightened and wondered what would happen if he let go of the guilt completely. If he accepted his father was the one solely responsible for losing the estate, that as a lad of eighteen there was absolutely nothing he could have done differently. It lifted that sense of duty, that sense of responsibility. Perhaps this was what his mother meant when she had told him not to let his pride ruin everything.

He blamed himself for the misery of everyone in Ballachulish and as such he wanted to be the only person to solve the issue. Instead of reaching out and asking for help, he had held the problem close, determined that he would be the one to resolve everything.

If he conceded he was not responsible for the selling of the Thomson family estate, he could consider things more rationally. Instead of being honour-bound to regain every last parcel of land he had lost, he could focus on really helping those most in need. Although it would be nice to get back Taigh Blath, he did not need it. He would be happy in a little cottage in the village, just as long as he had Selina by his side.

Selina. He had messed everything up there. He loved her and she loved him, but despite that she was still planning on leaving. She had seen well before him that his obsession with restoring his family's lands was going to destroy anything they could share.

Callum breathed deeply, taking in large lungfuls of the fresh air. He crouched down and dug his fingers into the dirt, taking a great handful of it, picking it up and then turning his palm over and letting the dirt run through his fingers. He repeated the action a few times, trying to ground himself, to connect his body with the land he loved dearly.

'You've been a pig-headed fool,' he murmured to himself.

An idea was beginning to form, a way forward that would take compromise, but would allow him to be happy.

Rising up, he looked once more at the view. First he needed to see Selina, to explain everything to her, to grovel for not being the man she had needed a few hours earlier. This last year she had been rejected by her father, kept close enough to control, but shown no real affection. No wonder she had decided to push Callum away. He should have declared his undying love for her loud and clear for everyone to hear, not asked her to wait with uncertainty while he tried to arrange everything to his advantage. She deserved more. She deserved to be somebody's everything.

'My everything,' Callum said.

He just hoped she would forgive him.

Chapter Twenty-One

'She left about an hour ago,' Shaun Fettle said. He was a young boy who worked at the Lost Sheep, clearing the tables and making whatever gristly stew was on the menu for the day. He was only about fourteen, tall and gangly with a shock of dark hair.

'She left?'

'Aye. After that snooty cow from Taigh Blath came to see her. Miss Shepherd came and settled her bill after and asked the best way to get to Glasgow to catch the coach to London.'

'She's only been here a few hours.'

Shaun shrugged, as if it were none of his business.

'What did you tell her? About how to get to Glasgow?'

'I told her my brother was taking the cart to Oban today ready for the market tomorrow and he wouldn't object to a passenger as pretty as her.'

Callum turned and left immediately. An hour's

head start was not much, especially when they were travelling in Thomas Fettle's rickety old cart with his ancient horse in the bridle, but he didn't like the idea of Selina getting further and further away from him.

He walked briskly to the large house a couple of miles away where Bruce lived and rapped on the door, surprised when the big man opened the door himself.

'Can I borrow one of your horses?'

'Of course. Has that canny lass run away from you?'

'Aye. Somehow I have driven her away, but I am eager to fix my mistakes.'

'I am glad to hear it. Let's get Bessie saddled and you on your way.'

'Thank you, Bruce. You are a true friend. I have something I need to discuss with you later, a business proposition, but first I need to go and ask Selina for forgiveness.'

'Settle the matters of the heart first and then matters of business later. Finally, I think you might be seeing sense.'

Bruce quickly saddled his horse, watching as Callum mounted.

'Good luck on your quest.'

Callum nodded his thanks and then urged Bessie

forward, finally feeling as though he were moving in the right direction.

He knew the road to Oban well as it twisted through some of the prettiest scenery of the Highlands. It was a mild day with the sun sometimes peeking out from behind the clouds and a gentle breeze to keep him from overheating. If he was not so preoccupied with what he was going to say to Selina, he would have enjoyed the ride.

After about an hour on the road he caught sight of a dust cloud up ahead and felt his pulse quicken in anticipation. He could not see the cart yet, but did not think there was likely going to be any other coach or carriage travelling on this road to Oban.

Ten minutes later he was close enough to call out, but he kept quiet, instead spurring the horse forward into a canter to cover the last of the remaining ground.

Thomas Fettle raised a hand in greeting, pulling his cart to the edge of the road, obviously thinking Callum wanted to go past. Next to him Selina sat with her hands folded demurely in her lap. For a moment she did not look up, but then she lifted her eyes to meet his and he saw she had been crying.

'I need to speak to Miss Shepherd, Thomas,' Callum said. 'I don't want to delay your journey, I know it is still a long way to Oban.'

'Callum…' Selina said, forgetting about the rules of Society in her distress and calling him by his given name.

'Please, my love. I really need to speak to you. I promise if you still wish to leave I will escort you to Oban myself.'

She hesitated and Thomas Fettle leaned over to murmur in her ear. Callum caught the end of the sentence.

'…choice, Miss.'

It felt like the longest wait ever as Selina bit her lip and looked at him, her eyes seeming to search his soul. Eventually she nodded and climbed down from the cart, as Callum dismounted.

'Thank you,' he said to her quietly. 'Thank you for giving me a chance.'

'Do you want me to wait, Miss?'

'No, that's very kind of you, Mr Fettle, but I do not wish to delay your journey to Oban. Thank you for all your kindness today.'

The young man touched the brim of his hat and then gave a flick of the reins, signalling for his ancient horse to start walking forward.

'You should be at Taigh Blath now, sorting everything out with Sir William.'

'I don't want to be there, I want to be with you. I always want to be with you, Selina.'

She grimaced. 'We spoke of this, Callum—it is one thing to want something, quite another for it to be practical.'

'Will you give me a chance to talk, to explain?' He took her hand, running his over her knuckles. 'Please, Selina.'

'You'll take me to Oban after?'

'I'll escort you all the way to Glasgow if you decide to go.'

'There's no need for that.'

'I hope not,' he said, smiling at her softly. 'I hope you'll be coming home with me.'

'You are too charming for your own good, Callum Thomson,' Selina said, unable to suppress the little smile that tugged at the corners of her lips.

Callum tied Bruce's horse up to a nearby tree a little off the road and took Selina by the hand again.

'How do you feel about forgiveness?'

'My vicar back home would say it is a noble act to forgive someone.'

'What if that person has been a massive fool?'

'I harbour no grudge towards you, Callum,' Selina said, sadness in her eyes. 'We were just two people who fell in love and could not resist the physical intimacy that came with it.'

Callum recoiled slightly. 'I am not apologising for *that*,' he said, shaking his head. 'When we are married we will make love so many times every single week that the one time we did it out of wedlock will be a miniscule proportion and barely worth thinking about.' He leaned in closer so his lips almost touched her ear. 'Although now I am thinking about it.'

'What are you apologising for, then?'

'For not falling to my knees immediately and asking you—no, begging you to marry me at the first opportunity. I love you, Selina.'

'I know, Callum, and I love you, too, but I am not the most important thing in your life. I am not what you want to fight for.'

'I am sorry I ever made you feel like that. You deserve to be worshipped. I know these last couple of years have been difficult, losing your mother and then being treated so terribly by your father. You deserve a relationship where you are celebrated, where you are beloved, not hidden away.'

'You can't give me that.'

'Please give me a chance. Let me show you I can.'

'What has changed since this morning, Callum?'

'I took a walk up above the forest, to a spot where you can see for miles. You can see the loch and the forest and the land that the Thomson family used to own. You can see the village and Taigh Blath…' he paused '... Loch View Lodge,' he corrected himself. The house was not something he thought he would ever get back and it would be better to start the process of letting it go.

'I realised that for a very long time I have been carrying a lot of guilt for things that I was not responsible for, things I had no control over. The importance of ancestral lands is drummed into us from a very young age. Even though I knew it was my father's actions that put us into awful debt, I was the one who signed the papers, who handed over the keys to Taigh Blath, who signed away the rights to the tenant farms and the houses in the village.'

'It wasn't your fault.'

'No, I know. But for a very long time I have secretly felt it was. My friends, my mother, they have been gently trying to suggest perhaps I have taken on too much of the responsibility for the loss of the land, but I am afraid the message never got through. It took losing you to realise I was the one making all the trouble for myself.'

'I'm glad you've realised that,' Selina said, looking genuinely pleased for him. 'But it does not change the fact that if we marry Sir William will take out his anger on the people of Ballachulish.'

'Perhaps not.'

'He will. He's a vindictive man.'

'I agree, but he is a man of business first, emotion second. If he is hit with a proposition that is beneficial to him, he will find it hard to say no because of a grudge.'

'You can't afford to buy the entirety of the estate from him—that was why you agreed to the marriage to Catherine in the first place.'

'I can't buy all the estate, but I can buy some of it. Not the house or the grounds, or much of the farmland, but I can buy the tenant cottages in Ballachulish. I have enough saved for that.'

He saw the flicker of interest in Selina's eyes. 'You could buy part of the estate?'

'Yes. I think I had this picture in my mind of the triumphant lord, returning in glory to restore all that had been lost in one swoop. I wanted people to hear the Thomson family name and think of how the estate had been, the tenants secure in their homes, not the drunkard of a lord who lost it all and the green boy who could not keep hold of his inheritance.' He shook his head. 'My mother told me pride was my downfall and she was right. I couldn't see that I didn't need to do everything, I just needed to do the right thing.'

Selina looked at him and for a moment he couldn't tell what she was thinking.

'Tell me your plan,' she said and in that instant he felt his heart soar. She was interested, invested in his plan and it meant he had succeeded in the first step of winning her round.

'Part one,' he said. 'We get married. There is no need for the pomp that you English require for your marriage, we could find a minister and tell him we wish to wed.'

'This is an integral part of your plan?'

'No,' he said with a grin, 'But I would like to be married to you so I thought I'd slip it in there.'

'Tell me part two,' Selina said, pressing her lips together to suppress a smile. He liked how she did that, as if she thought she should remain serious, but the smile tried to break through anyway.

'Part two is I gather the people of Ballachulish as well as a few landowners I trust from the local area. I am going to suggest that we put together what funds we have to form a group that hopefully has enough to buy the tenant farms as well as the houses in Ballachulish. We draw up a contract that stipulates fairly everyone's contribution and the percentage ownership they have of all the properties. Any rents collected will be fair and just and will be divided as per the ratios in the document.'

'You then have to get Sir William to agree to this.'

'I will do my best to persuade him. He will be leaving Scotland without the marriage he wanted for Miss Kingsley, but I get the impression he is not enamoured with our country anyway. This way he gets to be free of the troublesome parts of the estate and keeps only the house and estate grounds. He can tell all his London friends he has a property in Scotland, but he does not have to worry about collecting rents or arguing over contracts with tenant farmers.'

'He might accept your proposition,' Selina said, but she didn't sound convinced. 'But you will not have Taigh Blath. You will not have the estate that was promised to you from birth.'

'And perhaps,' he said quietly, looking out into the distance, 'that is exactly what I deserve. I should have stopped being so selfish earlier and used the funds I did have to buy back what I could, rather than holding on to them in the hope that I might be able to have everything, when all the while people were suffering and I almost lost the woman I loved.'

'You would stay here in Ballachulish?'

'Yes,' he said firmly. 'If my beautiful young wife could bear to live in a simple cottage.'

Selina did not say anything and Callum found himself holding his breath. He knew the living situation would not be an issue for Selina. She had not grown up in luxury and had hinted at how her family had often struggled to get by. They had rented a set of rooms in St Leonards-on-Sea where Selina said the best thing about them was the view from the top window of the sea. What he was more concerned about was whether she would accept his apology.

'You truly would not resent me if you could not gain back all of what your father lost?'

'No. I would give thanks every day that I had such a wonderful wife and that I had not reneged on the promise I made to the people of Ballachulish. I have come to realise the rest does not matter. I am still the Earl, but truly what does it matter if I live in Taigh Blath or if I live in a cosy little cottage in the village?'

He paused. 'I am sorry, Selina, for making this so hard. You are the most incredible woman I have ever met and you deserve to be celebrated. I did not see I was adding to the hurt your father had dealt you by not realising how important the love we share is.' He looked her deeply in the eyes. 'If you say yes, then I will spend each and every day showing you how important you are to me.'

Selina turned to face him fully and flung her arms around him, tears spilling on to her cheeks.

'Does this mean you'll marry me?'

'Yes. Of course I'll marry you. Although not today.'

'I thought that might be pushing my luck a little.'

'I want our wedding to be a celebration. I am done with hiding who I am from the world.'

'Then we will ask the local minister to read the banns so it can be announced for the whole world to hear and then we will arrange the biggest celebration this village has ever seen.'

'I would be happy with another dance in the barn.'

He kissed her, feeling his heart swell. 'Of course you would. *That* was the night you fell in love with me.'

Selina scoffed. 'You could tell, I suppose.'

He shrugged. 'I knew you liked me before then and it obvious you lusted after me.'

'*Lusted* after you?' Selina cried out, shaking her head at his audacity.

'Deny it.'

She pressed her lips together, but avoided his eye, unable to deny it.

'But I think it was that night, when all your anger towards me fizzled out, that you fell in love with me.'

'And when did you fall in love with me?'

'I told you, that first night we met on the edge of the loch. I felt as though something monumental in my life had just changed and I fell in love a little more each time I saw you.'

She lifted up on her tiptoes and kissed him and he wondered how he had ever thought his life could be complete without the woman in his arms.

'Will Bruce's horse be able to carry both of us?' she asked as he unhooked the reins from the tree.

'Aye, as long as we take it slow. At a walk we'll

be back in Ballachulish before sundown. I will call a meeting tonight and tomorrow I will go to Sir William with the proposal.'

'Lady Kingsley still thinks you are going to marry Catherine. She came to see me earlier and gave me the money for my journey south, on the condition I left immediately and didn't come back.' Selina allowed Callum to boost her up on to the horse's back and settled on the area in front of the saddle. 'It is not a promise I am desperate to keep.'

Callum launched himself up behind her and they set off at a gentle pace, back the way they had come, but now with Selina's body resting against his. He felt contented, as if all was right in the world finally.

Chapter Twenty-Two

As they stood hand in hand outside Taigh Blath, Selina felt a knot forming in her stomach. She had insisted on coming along, wanting to face her father one final time before hopefully never seeing him again. She also had a little plan of her own that she had not told Callum about, some leverage that she hoped to use if the negotiations were not going their way.

Yesterday evening, on returning to Ballachulish, Callum had recruited a group of young men to go and knock on everyone's doors and call them to a meeting in the big barn where they'd held their illicit dance. Callum had spoken with passion and authority, his demeanour humble, but also that of a man who wanted to take charge.

The villagers had been overwhelming in their support and a few of the wealthier residents who owned their own homes had come forward to pledge some small amounts of money to help the cause. The people who really mattered, in a practical rather than emotional sense, were the local landowners, though. Selina had watched, hands clasped together nervously, as they had listened to Callum's proposal with expressionless faces. She had not been able to gauge their reaction until Callum had finished talking.

There was silence and then after ten seconds a farmer who owned a few acres and ran a relatively successful dairy farm stood up and clapped. He had declared it was about time they acted and he was all too happy to help secure the future of the people of Ballachulish, the people he'd grown up with and considered his friends.

Bruce had put forward a large amount of money, second only to Callum's own pot. It was almost everything he had earned while in Canada, minus a few pounds he had kept back to ensure he had enough funds for the wedding. Between Callum and Bruce and the other smaller landowners, Callum calculated there was enough to buy a large portion of the estate back from Sir William. Now all they needed to do was convince him to sell.

'Good morning,' a footman said, peering out into the fog before taking a step back in surprise as he saw Callum and Selina standing there. 'I am not sure...'

'If we are welcome here? No, I expect we are not, but it is vital we speak to Sir William.'

'I will go and enquire as to whether he will receive you.'

'He won't receive us,' Selina murmured, her hand slipping a little further up Callum's arm. She wanted to be brave and bold, but every moment they stood outside, waiting to be dismissed, she felt more and more like the girl who had been scorned and belittled by her father for a year before realising she was worth more. Deciding to make things different, she tugged at Callum's arm. 'Come on. He can't refuse to see us if we're already in his study.'

She marched inside, aware she might be tackled to the ground at any moment by an irate Catherine or a furious Lady Kingsley. Selina did not slow or stop until she reached the door of her father's study. She could hear the murmur of voices inside, no doubt as the footman assured Sir William he was not lying, that Callum and Selina were both outside.

'Father,' she said as she strode into the room, 'You look tired. I hope you are well.'

'Get out,' he said, rising from his desk. He took two steps towards her before he saw Callum, tall and broad in the doorway. Sir William was prideful man, but he was also clever. He knew there was no way he would ever win in a physical fight against Callum, so he did not even try.

'Lord Leven,' he said, looking Callum up and

down, a little smile now playing on his lips 'I understand from my daughter you have been a busy man.'

'We ask for a few minutes of your time. I have a proposition that I think you will appreciate.'

'What makes you think I would ever consider doing business with you? You have shown yourself to be untrustworthy and unreliable. I should have known there was a reason you lost your entire estate, your entire birthright.'

Selina glanced at Callum, aware of how sensitive a topic this was for him, even now, but she was pleased to see he looked in control of himself.

From behind them there was a squeal of frustration and then Catherine barrelled into the room, looking more like a child than the demure young woman she was meant to be.

'What is *she* doing here?'

Lady Kingsley followed, her eyes blazing. 'You gave me your word you were leaving and never coming back. I should have known not to trust the word of a bastard child like you.'

Callum held up a hand, his voice low but clear, cutting through the frenzied mood in the room.

'Please refrain from attacking Miss Shepherd. I had hoped to come here today to settle some of the bad feeling between my family and yours, Sir William, but I will not tolerate Miss Shepherd being treated poorly.'

'You stand by her, then?' Sir William asked, his eyes fixed on Selina. 'You do know she has nothing to offer you, no dowry, no family connections?'

'I know everything,' Callum said. Sir William fell silent, no doubt assessing how much damage Callum could do to him with the knowledge that Selina was Sir William's illegitimate daughter.

'Sit down. I will listen to what you have to stay.'

'Father...' wailed Catherine.

'Either conduct yourself with an appropriate level of decorum or leave,' Sir William snapped at his younger daughter.

Lady Kingsley and Catherine both fell silent, perching on the window seat just in Selina's eyeline.

Selina and Callum took the two seats in front of the large desk while Sir William returned to his chair behind it.

'I want to start with an apology,' Callum said, speaking clearly and calmly. 'I am sorry our negotiations stalled and ultimately failed. When you made the journey up here to Scotland I was hopeful of a union between our families.' He turned to Catherine, his voice soft. 'I apologise to you as well, Miss Kingsley. You are a very eligible young lady and I know one day you will find the right man to be your husband.'

'You cannot mean to marry her,' Lady Kingsley said, the words spilling from her despite Sir William's look of admonishment. 'You would choose Selina over my Catherine?'

'Miss Shepherd and I are very much in love and you cannot argue with love.'

'You are a fool,' Sir William snapped. 'No one of consequence marries for love.'

'There we will have to disagree,' Callum said, taking hold of Selina's hand and lifting it into his lap. 'You met my mother. I expect you know her lineage. She is second cousin to the Prince Regent. She has a connection to almost every member of the London *ton* despite not having been back to England for years. She is an advocate for love matches—I understand they are gaining popularity among the upper echelons of Society.'

Sir William did not have an answer for this so Callum pushed on.

'I love your daughter Miss Shepherd,' he clarified quickly. 'We will be wed as soon as the proper arrangements have been made.'

'What about me?' Catherine asked, her voice barely more than a whisper. 'I was meant to marry the Earl. I was meant to be mistress of a Scottish estate. Not her.'

Selina looked down at her lap. Despite everything Catherine had put her through over the last year she had never set out to hurt her half-sister. Although she had only ever been cruel to Selina, perhaps once she was out in the world, hopefully married to a decent man, she might well lose some of the spitefulness and become someone Selina could get along with.

'You said you had a proposition for me,' Sir William said, unwilling to congratulate the couple on their upcoming nuptials. 'I am not inclined to be generous, given the havoc you have wrought in our lives, but I will listen if you are quick.'

'I expect you are keen to get back to England. You will have missed most of the Season, but there are summer parties, no doubt, and next Season to prepare for.'

Sir William narrowed his eyes and regarded Callum. Selina knew her father and his family were not invited to all the big events of the Season. It was what had driven them here to Scotland, this quest to be accepted by the highest in Society. Sir William looked as though he could not decide if there was a barbed insult in the comment or merely ignorance.

'We shall be returning to England soon,' Sir William confirmed.

'I would like to buy some of the land and estate from you before you go. It will leave you with less to manage. It is a long way from England to Scotland and I cannot imagine it is easy having property so far away.'

'You cannot afford to buy back the entirety of the estate,' Sir William said. 'And I am disinclined to give you favourable rates. You have cost me enough with this wasted trip.'

'I do not wish for the whole estate—you are right, I cannot afford it. You can keep Loch View Lodge and the grounds. I want to buy the rest.'

Sir William frowned, clearly not expecting this.

Callum continued. 'It would allow you to still tell people you had an extensive estate in the Scottish Highlands, bought off the impoverished Thomson family, but not have to worry about managing the locals.'

'You don't want the house?'

Callum shrugged and Selina felt the tension in his body beside her despite his best efforts to disguise it.

'As you say, I can't afford everything. Loch View Lodge has been in my family for generations, for hundreds of years, but it is not my priority right now.'

'You want the farmland and the houses in the village? Why? They hardly generate a huge income.' Sir

William's eyes narrowed. 'Unless you plan to turn the land over to sheep.'

'No,' Callum said, trying not to let on how much the idea disgusted him. 'I wish to manage the farmland and rent out the properties, that is all.'

Sir William tapped his fingers on the edge of his chair, contemplating Callum's proposal.

'You cannot be thinking of doing a deal with this man,' Lady Kingsley said, unable to contain herself any longer.

'Quiet. I'm thinking.'

'He has brought disgrace on our darling daughter Catherine.'

Callum turned in his chair to face Lady Kingsley. 'Again, I apologise, but there is not really any need for this to affect your daughter's prospects. I do not plan on gracing the London Season with my presence. To those who know you were making this trip to finalise a marriage deal you can spread the story that the match was unsuitable. Paint me as a penniless Scottish rogue. A barbarian if you wish. They will lap that up in London. You can tell everyone you were the ones to pull out of the agreement. No one will know any different.'

Lady Kingsley looked as though she might argue, but closed her mouth again as she considered Callum's words. She would not concede she was in any way pleased with how events had turned out, but Callum was right, it did not have to reflect badly on Catherine.

'You would not contradict any story we put about?'

'No. As long as you did not say anything negative about my new wife. I really am rather protective of her.'

'We do not wish to draw any attention to Miss Shepherd,' Sir William said, flicking a disdainful look at Selina.

'Good. So what do you think of my proposal, Sir William? You get to keep the pleasant parts of the estate, I buy the working parts from you.'

Selina could see he was considering it, despite the animosity still in the room.

'Very well,' he said eventually. 'I will give you a price.'

The tension in the room was palpable as the only sound was the scratching of Sir William's pen on a piece of paper he pulled from a drawer. He pushed it across the desk towards Callum and then flicked Selina a spiteful little smile.

She leaned in to Callum as he picked up the piece of paper. 'It is going to be far more than the land is worth,' she whispered. 'Do you trust me?'

He glanced at her and then nodded before opening

up the paper. On it was a figure treble what Callum and the other local landowners had raised.

Selina took the piece of paper from Callum's hand, her heart pounding in her chest. It was all very well thinking she would stand up to her father when she was far from his searching gaze, but sitting right here in front of him was a different matter.

'That is a ridiculous amount.' Selina took the piece of paper from Callum and flicked it back at her father.

'That is the price I am willing to sell it to Lord Leven for. If he does not like it…' Sir William spread his hands out in front of him and shrugged.

'You are going to offer him fair price,' Selina said.

'That is not how this works,' Sir William snarled.

'It is. I might not have a voice at the moment, but in a few weeks I will be Lady Leven, Countess of Leven. My husband may have no desire to travel to London, but I did not find the journey here arduous. I would be welcomed as Lord Leven's new wife into the very ballrooms and dining rooms you covet an invitation to and then I would start talking.' She slammed both her hands down on the desk in front of her and then smiled sweetly. 'I do not know what I would say first. Certainly the ladies and gentlemen would hear what a scoundrel you were, how you were not to be trusted. Gossip spreads like fire and I could create enough gossip about you to last three lifetimes.'

'You dare to blackmail me?'

'I dare. Perhaps I have learnt something from you. Perhaps the last twelve months have not been a complete waste of time after all.'

'I will not lower the price.'

'I suppose I *have* been listening this past year. You do have such a loud voice, Father, and you did ask me to stay in the house all the time. A young woman can hardly be blamed for overhearing a few conversations in her own home.'

Sir William paled slightly, but still did not concede defeat. 'You have nothing.'

'I could contact Mr Warrington and...' Selina began, but Sir William stood, grabbing the piece of paper and crossing out the number he had written. He wrote something else and flung it across the desk at her. Aware the ink was still wet, Selina picked it up carefully and gave it to Callum.

She watched his face as he read the new number, wondering if she would have to carry on.

'We have a deal, Sir William.' Callum looked serious but Selina could sense inside he was celebrating.

'Not quite,' she said, to the surprise of everyone in the room. 'I have one more request. I would like a wedding present from my father. You gave me nothing the first twenty-two years of my life so I would like a wedding present now.'

'No.'

Selina shrugged. 'Consider it,' she said, sitting back down in her chair as if she had all the time in the world. 'If you agree, our relationship will end on a much sweeter note.'

'I do not care about our relationship.'

'That much is very clear, Father. Let me explain.' She took Callum's hand but held her father's gaze. 'As a wedding present I would like you to give us this house and the land that accompanies it. I know Lord Leven said he was not interested in purchasing it, but *I* do wish to obtain it. It will be a gift to Lord Leven and me, separate from the other deal you have made. No money will exchange hands.'

'You will not threaten me endlessly.'

'This is not a threat. It is an offer. As I said before, I will be Lady Leven, Countess. My sister—' she glanced at Catherine '—my true sister, is happily married to Lord Routledge. She is a viscountess, which is impressive of itself, but perhaps more importantly Lord Routledge is quite one of the most influential men in London.' Selina was beginning to enjoy herself now and she threw the next comment over her shoulder to Lady Kingsley. 'You have to admit that is not bad for two illegitimate nobodies from a tiny town in Sussex.'

'You don't need to do this,' Callum murmured as Selina paused for breath, but she could see he was captivated, as invested as the rest of them in her speech.

'Either we could part on bad terms, which could mean a cold shoulder from anyone who knows Lord Routledge, or we could forge an alliance.'

'You do not want an alliance with these people,' Callum cautioned her.

Selina glanced from Sir William to Lady Kingsley and back again. She was gambling here. Although so far she had not lied—her sister was happily married to Lord Routledge—they were not the darlings of the *ton* at present. They had escaped to a quiet life at the seaside soon after they married. It had all happened around about the time Sir William and his family had left London, so Selina was hoping they had not heard anything of their eschewing Society events.

'My sister and I will launch Catherine into Society. We will even pretend she is some distant relative. She will get a Season, hopefully attract an eligible suitor and the door to what you want most of all will be opened for you.'

Nobody spoke and Selina could see this was not what they had expected.

'I have a few conditions. I cannot cope with you…' she pointed at Lady Kingsley '…or you…' another finger pointed at her father. 'You would stay away until Catherine had a suitor ready and waiting to ask for her hand. Then I could slip away without having to spend any time with you.'

Still nobody spoke and Selina wondered if her idea was that terrible. She didn't really want to spend a whole six months with Catherine, but if it meant Callum got his ancestral home back she would put up with it.

'How could I trust you?'

'A contract, just like the land contract,' Selina said with a shrug. 'Prepared by a solicitor and signed by both parties. You gift us the house, we agree to launch Catherine into Society in London.'

'A Season? A London Season?' Catherine's eyes were wide, but she moved quickly over to the desk. 'You have to say yes, Papa. Think of the man I could marry if I had a proper London Season.'

'You know nothing of launching a woman into Society. You have never even met the Queen yourself.'

'No, but as I say it would not just be me. Lord and Lady Routledge would assist if I asked them to.'

Sir William frowned, trying to work out the advantages and disadvantages of this one.

Finally, to Selina's surprise he stood and held out his hand for Callum to shake.

'You have a deal. The land for the sum written down. The house and grounds in exchange for a London Season for Catherine.'

Callum took Sir William's hand and shook it. Selina felt like crying out with relief. Her hands had started to shake, but she did not want anyone to see so quickly she hid them in her skirt.

'I will summon a solicitor from Glasgow. When he arrives we will finalise the details.'

Before anyone could change their minds Selina and Callum said brief farewells and hurried from the room, pausing only once they were outside the front door.

'You never let on you were going to ask for all that,' Callum said, pulling her to him and kissing her deeply. 'Remind me never to negotiate with you—you are far too skilled for us mere mortals.'

'I'm sorry I promised we would go to London, I know you have no desire to leave Scotland.'

'I don't, but I am learning it is good to not hold on to my rigid ideas. London is the price we must pay to come back to this beautiful house.'

'We should go and tell the villagers that Sir William accepted your offer. They will be relieved.'

'We will,' Callum said. 'But first I need to kiss my clever wife.'

Standing on the steps of the home they would one day soon move back to, he kissed her long and hard until Selina forgot about the conflict with her father and the promises she'd had to make to get the deal they wanted, until all she could think about was the man she loved and their wonderful future together.

Epilogue

Selina slipped her hand into the crook of her sister's elbow and stepped closer. Sarah had arrived in Ballachulish five days earlier and Selina felt a contentment that she hadn't in a long time. All her favourite people in the world were gathered here around her.

'This is beautiful, Selina. I can't believe you live here.'

'I can't believe you returned to St Leonards.'

Sarah sighed. 'Do you know, it was the happiest few months. Although we did not have much money, it was just Henry, his sister Sophia and I, until little Rupert came along. We worked hard, I even took in some pupils and taught them to play the piano. There is something to be said about the simple life. Everything has changed now. Henry's horrible father died and now Henry is the Earl. It is a lot of responsibility, of course, but it is nice to live without wondering what he might do to try to tear us apart.'

Selina smiled suddenly. 'It's a common theme, isn't it, with us—horrible fathers. Henry's was controlling, Callum's a terrible drunk and ours manipulative and cruel.'

'At least our children will have better,' Sarah said, squeezing Selina's hand and then glancing down at her sister's belly.

Sarah and Henry had not made it in time for the wedding. Despite Selina's initial desire to wait for a large celebration of their love, the reality of waiting week after week had been too difficult so in the end they'd had a small ceremony followed by a huge party with everyone in Ballachulish invited. Sarah had travelled as soon as she was able with little Rupert.

'We need you ladies,' Callum called out from where he was standing at the edge of the lawn. 'We need an independent judge.'

Selina broke away from her sister and ran over, kissing Callum on the lips as he picked her up and twirled her around. She felt the material of his kilt flare a little and as always it made her smile. Long gone was the man who thought he did not deserve to wear the tartan of his ancestors and now he wore his kilt at even a hint of a special occasion.

'Ah, newlyweds,' Henry said, shaking his head. 'Do you remember when we were that young and in love?' He grabbed hold of his wife and picked her up, kissing her deeply.

'How are my darling wife and beautiful baby?' Callum said, laying a hand on Selina's bump.

'Thriving, my darling. Now, what do you need us for?'

'Now, Routledge has excellent aim, as you can see.' He motioned at the tree a few feet in front of them. 'For a man who tells me he has never thrown an axe before I am amazed, but would we say that was in the centre of the tree?'

Selina rolled her eyes. 'Has dear Henry bested you at your own sport?'

'Hardly,' Callum said and gave her a wink. 'And if he has I blame the hard labour I was toiling away at yesterday. My arm does feel a little stiff.'

'Mrs Murray told me about your efforts to rebuild the little wall in their garden. She was bemused that the Earl was getting his hands dirty.'

'I need to protect our investment, Selina. It is not only my money involved.'

Since the group of local landowners had bought the land and properties from Sir William the village had thrived. People who had moved away were coming back and Callum was always producing ideas to try to increase the amount of work in the area or the yield from the farms. There was a great sense of community and they were at the centre of it.

She walked over to the tree and studied the axe. 'I would say it was pretty central.'

Callum cursed under his breath and then clapped Henry on the back. 'Well done, Routledge. Perhaps we'll get you started as a lumberjack while you're here.'

'I handle axes for pleasure only,' Henry said, making Sarah laugh.

Together they all walked back towards Taigh Blath. It was an early autumn day and the light made the house glow.

'I feel very lucky,' Selina said as she and Callum paused outside the front door. 'I have my wonderful sister to stay and my gorgeous nephew. The perfect house, in the perfect village. And I have you.' She raised herself up on her tiptoes and kissed Callum, unable to believe that just a few short months ago she had never even set foot in Scotland, let alone thought she might fall in love with a Scottish laird.

* * * * *

MILLS & BOON®

Coming next month

COURTING SCANDAL WITH THE DUKE
Ann Lethbridge

His ire rose once more. 'Listen to me, you little fool, you are one whisper away from ruin. Do you not understand this?'

She backed up until the trunk halted her progress, clearly surprised by his anger.

She frowned at him. 'What does it matter to you?'

What indeed? It shouldn't matter at all, but for some reason it did. 'You asked me for advice. Now I am giving it.'

'Then what are you suggesting?'

'It all depends on whether or not you were recognised.' He removed his hat and ran a hand through his hair. 'Why the devil would anyone think going to a gentleman's club would not be a problem?'

Defiance filled her gaze. A dare. A challenge. 'In Paris a lady is welcome everywhere.'

He stepped closer, forcing her to raise her gaze to his face, reminding her that for all that she was tall, he was taller. Larger.

Her soft lips parted on a breath. Her eyelids dropped a fraction. Her chest rose and fell with short sharp breaths.

His heart pounded in his chest. His blood, a moment before warm with anger, now ran like fire through his veins. Desire.

Only by ironclad will did he restrain from unbearable temptation.

'I—'

She raised her palm, face out as if holding him at bay. He took a breath.

Her hand pressed against his chest, then slid upwards, around his nape, and she went up on tiptoes and pressed her mouth to his.

Luscious, soft lips moving slowly.

He pulled her close, responding to her touch in a blinding instant, ravishing her mouth, stroking her back, pulling her close and hard against his body.

For a moment his mind was blank, but his body was alive as it had never been before. Out of control.

Continue reading

COURTING SCANDAL WITH THE DUKE
Ann Lethbridge

Available next month
millsandboon.co.uk

Copyright © 2025 Michéle Ann Young

COMING SOON!

We really hope you enjoyed reading this book.
If you're looking for more romance
be sure to head to the shops when
new books are available on

Thursday 25th September

To see which titles are coming soon, please visit
millsandboon.co.uk/nextmonth

MILLS & BOON

MILLS & BOON TRUE LOVE IS HAVING A MAKEOVER!

Introducing

Love Always

Swoon-worthy romances, where love takes center stage. Same heartwarming stories, stylish new look!

Look out for our brand new look
COMING SEPTEMBER 2025
MILLS & BOON

FOUR BRAND NEW BOOKS FROM
MILLS & BOON MODERN

Indulge in desire, drama, and breathtaking romance – where passion knows no bounds!

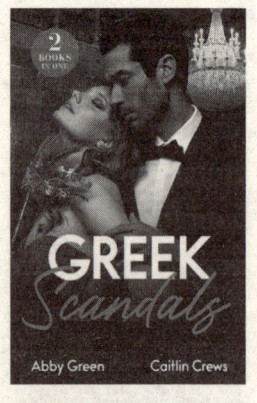

OUT NOW

Eight Modern stories published every month, find them all at:

millsandboon.co.uk